THE ELSEWHERE EMPORIUM

ROSS MACKENZIE

Kelpies

Kelpies is an imprint of Floris Books
First published in 2018 by Floris Books
© 2018 Ross MacKenzie

The publisher acknowledges subsidy from
Creative Scotland towards the publication
of this volume

 Also available as an eBook

British Library CIP data available
ISBN 978-178250-519-8
Printed in Poland

To Derek and Shona,
and clear skies ahead.

PROLOGUE

THE MAN IN THE CRIMSON SCARF

Mayfair, London, 1967

There was, or so it seemed, nothing unusual about the house on Park Street.

Like the adjoining buildings, Number 120 was tall and narrow and made of red brick. It was grand without being gaudy, stern without seeming cold. The window frames were clean and white, the door shining black. There were no plants in the windows, no brightly coloured curtains. Sitting in the middle of a row of identical dwellings, it seemed that there could have been no place in the world more average or uninteresting.

Which was exactly what they wanted you to think.

It was not uncommon for long stretches to pass without so much as a flicker of movement from Number 120. No comings or goings. But if you were inclined to watch for long enough a time, weeks perhaps, or months, eventually your patience would pay off.

Eventually, you would see the man in the crimson scarf.

Our story begins on a cold October night. London wore an autumn coat the colour of moonlight and the air was perfumed with falling leaves and tingling with whispers of the approaching winter.

It was well past eleven o'clock when the man in the crimson scarf turned the corner onto Park Street. He was small – only a hair over five feet – and he wore a black suit and gloves and shoes. His eyes were dark, his neat beard silvery, and his skin smooth and pale as bone. The only bit of colour about him was the scarf of fine crimson silk thrown around his neck.

When the man approached Number 120 he stopped at the foot of the steps and cast his eye over the building. There he stood for some time, examining every brick, every pane of glass in every window. When he was satisfied, he climbed the steps. He put his ear to the fine black door, listening intently. Then he pulled his head away, removed one of his gloves, reached out and traced an invisible shape on the door with his finger. He popped the finger in his mouth and rolled the taste around.

Only when all of this was done did the man in the crimson scarf at last reach into the pocket of his coat, bring out a key, open the door and enter the house.

He closed the front door behind him softly and took off his coat and scarf. He hung them on an iron coat stand by the door, and turned to observe the hallway, painted in shades of shadow and dust. Inhaling deeply, the man smelled the cold emptiness of the tall house, the stale carpets and fabrics, the rotting wood, the dampness.

The man's mouth twitched very slightly at the corners. Not quite a smile, but almost. He reached into the pocket of his suit jacket and brought out a small, plain-looking book with black-edged pages and a black cover. When he held the book, it was small enough to sit comfortably in his palm, and it fell open at a particular passage. The book opened here because this text had been used many, many times before. The man in the crimson scarf himself had read these words countless times, and the fingerprints of his predecessors spanning generations were imprinted on those pages.

He ran a finger down the page, shook his head in appreciation of the craftsmanship. Every time he came upon a piece of magic such as this, which was rare to say the least, a part of him would sadden, because magicians these days just couldn't create magic this special any more. The art had gone out of it. This enchantment – and that's what it was, an enchantment – came from a rich era in the history of magic.

He read the enchantment aloud, his lips curling around the crisp words, and as he spoke the house filled with crackling energy. When he reached the final few words, he slowed and closed his eyes, relishing every syllable.

Silence.

Eyes still shut, he breathed in and found that the smells of the empty house, the damp and dust, were gone, replaced by a cocktail of aromas: burning oil lamps and lush, thick carpet, polished wood and a crackling coal fire.

"Hem hem."

The man in the scarf opened his eyes. He smiled, as he did every time he witnessed the results of the enchantment.

The house had transformed.

Where there had been shadow, there was now golden lamplight. Where there had been dust and torn wallpaper, broken mirrors, fallen paintings, everything was now spick and span, rich and gleaming.

"Welcome back to the Bureau, Mr Ivy, sir. How was the journey?"

The man who had been wearing the crimson scarf, Mr Ivy, nodded to a butler who had appeared as if from nowhere. "Fine, thank you, Kenworth. How have things been here? Anything to report?"

Kenworth stood straight-backed and proper, his face dominated by a large, proud nose. He raised his bushy eyebrows.

"Oh, nothing much, Mr Ivy. The usual. A couple of moonghasts tried to nest in the attic and, as you can imagine, we had some trouble removing them. Thomas lost a finger, sir."

"The poor fellow!"

"Oh, it's quite alright, sir. Mrs Pennyworth gave him a dose of something or other and the finger grew back – though he swears it doesn't always do what he tells it. Are we expecting guests tonight, sir?"

"Ah. Yes. We are indeed, Kenworth."

"How many, sir?"

"Three."

Kenworth nodded. "I shall set the table immediately, sir."

"Thank you, Kenworth. Oh, but set it for two instead of three, will you? Mrs Hennypeck is coming, and the dead don't eat."

Mrs Hennypeck was dead. There was no disputing that fact. But being dead did not stop her from being the loudest person at the table. She was very tiny, with sharp, high cheekbones, and her grey hair was pinned high. She dressed impeccably, even if the style of her clothes had not been in fashion for many years. Around her neck she wore a distinctive necklace. Its powerful magic tethered her soul to her body and allowed her to remain in the world of the 'living', even after death.

"In my day," she gestured quite grandly around the room, "this house was filled with magicians. Dozens of us! All working cases, all solving magical crimes. The Bureau of Magical Investigation was a name that still struck fear into the hearts of the magical underworld!"

There were three people sitting around the table – Mr Ivy, the small, shrivelled figure of Mrs Hennypeck and a solemn ten-year-old boy with smooth ebony skin and striking green eyes. His name was Flintwitch, and he stared at the dead old woman with a mixture of wonder and grim fascination.

"Yes, well," Mr Ivy stripped the last of the meat from his prime rib with his teeth, "things certainly have changed since your day, Mrs Hennypeck."

"I'll say," the dead old woman continued. "I mean, there are only two of you! *Two!* And you, young man... how old are you? Six? You look barely out of nappies!"

"I'm ten," replied Flintwitch, looking quite put out. Before he could add something he might come to regret, Mr Ivy butted in.

"Flintwitch is a supremely talented young man, I assure you. And as for our lack of numbers… it's not through choice, Mrs Hennypeck. Nobody wants to join the Bureau these days. There's far too much money and glamour to be found in the freelance investigating scene. Nowadays, bounty hunters and monster trackers are plastered all over the covers of magazines and newspapers like they're movie stars! But you see, there are some cases that only the Bureau can handle. Some crimes that these glory-hunting celebrities will not touch. And that, Mrs Hennypeck, is why we have asked you back tonight. We need your help."

The dead old woman sat forward in her chair and drummed her pale-blue fingers on the surface of the table. The fire spat and popped.

"Go on."

Mr Ivy nodded to Flintwitch, and the boy reached under his chair and brought out a black leather briefcase. He opened the case and produced three photographs, sliding them across the table.

"Do you recognise anyone?"

Mrs Hennypeck stared down at the photos.

"Madge Branson." She pulled the faded photographs nearer. "And Godfrey Puddle. And that's Tobias Hook.

These people were my contemporaries – they worked for the Bureau when I did, lived in this very house…" The dead old woman looked up at her dining companions. "Has something happened to them?"

Flintwitch and Mr Ivy exchanged dark looks.

"I'm sorry to tell you," said Mr Ivy, "that over the past two weeks, the three magicians in question have vanished. We believe that they are dead, Mrs Hennypeck. Murdered."

"Murdered? Former Bureau Investigators *murdered?*"

Mrs Hennypeck brought her cold, dead little fist down on the table, causing the crockery to jump and Flintwitch to choke on a mouthful of candied pineapple.

As Flintwitch's face turned purple, the dining room door opened and Kenworth the butler wafted into the room. He stopped behind Flintwitch's chair, raised a hand, and slapped him hard on the back. The piece of candied pineapple shot out of Flintwitch's mouth and soared across the dining table. The butler gave a small bow and left the room once more.

"Sorry," said Flintwitch.

Mrs Hennypeck raised her eyebrows at Flintwitch before running a dead finger over the faces in the photographs.

"There are no bodies?"

"No," said Mr Ivy. "No bodies. But there are… circumstances."

"Someone or some*thing* is bumping off retired Bureau investigators." Flintwitch frowned and shook his head. "None of the big-shot freelancers out there will touch this. They're all scared stiff. It's really heavy."

Mrs Hennypeck gave him a confused look.

"Heavy? Are you having trouble lifting something, young man?"

"What? No… *Heavy*. Heavy! You know… it means really serious."

The dead old woman sighed in frustration. "Well, why on earth didn't you just say 'really serious' if that's what you meant?"

"It's slang, Mrs Hennypeck," said Mr Ivy.

She gave Flintwitch a disapproving look and sniffed. "Yes, well, being dead, I don't have much inclination to keep track of how today's youth are butchering the Queen's English."

Mr Ivy pinched the bridge of his nose and sighed. "The point is, Mrs Hennypeck, we invited you here tonight to ask if you might consider coming back to the Bureau temporarily. Your skills are legend and, I believe, if this killer continues their pattern, it will be of great benefit to have someone on board who has knowledge of the victims. So what do you say? Will you help us?"

Mrs Hennypeck considered this.

"Well, quite a lot of my time these days is taken up by being dead, but I must admit my old brain could use some exercise." She tapped the photographs. "And these were fine people, good magicians. They deserve justice."

She leaned over the table and offered a hand to Mr Ivy, who smiled and shook it with vigour. When it was Flintwitch's turn, he gasped at how cold and hard the old woman's hand was, but she merely gave him a wink and said, "Very well. Let's get to work. Tell me everything."

CHAPTER 1

THE CARNIVAL

Keswick, England, Present Day

"So? What do you think?"

Daniel Holmes pressed the palms of his hands together and bobbed up and down a little, his eyes fixed on Ellie Silver as she looked around. They were standing in the centre of an enormous fairground, colourful tents of every shape and size stretching off into the distance. The air smelled like toffee apples and candyfloss, and the evening sky was vast and cloudless, painting the city of tents in shades of dusk. All around, carnival workers and performers were busy juggling or stilt walking or doing one of a great many wonderful things.

Daniel had been changing things in the Nowhere Emporium slowly since he'd taken over six months ago. This was partly out of respect for Mr Silver, the former owner of the magical shop of Wonders – and Ellie's late father – and partly because the place was so unimaginably huge. Why, just the previous week he'd discovered a network of forgotten tunnels hidden under overgrown woodland that had burst out of one of the Emporium's rooms.

Ellie looked around, seemed to take everything in slowly. She sniffed the air, rolled the taste of the place around her mouth as if she was sampling some fine delicacy. She narrowed her eyes and ran a hand through her long black curls. She turned to Daniel.

He gulped.

"I like it."

It took a moment for her words to settle, but when they did, Daniel felt such a rush of relief and happiness that it seemed to inflate in him like a balloon. His shoulders, which had been gathered up around his ears somewhere, relaxed, and he bent over slightly, his hands on his thighs.

"You don't know how much it means to hear you say that!"

Ellie took a toffee apple from a passing fairground worker, sunk her teeth into it.

"You were frightened!" she said, spitting splinters of toffee at him.

"No," Daniel shrugged, "not frightened, just nervous. I mean, you've only ever known the Emporium to be one way – the way your dad made it. This is the first time I've changed anything… *big*."

Ellie put a hand on his shoulder. "Daniel, I miss Papa, and that's alright. It's normal. But just because he's not here any more doesn't mean that you shouldn't get on with your job. He left the shop to you. He'd be furious if he thought you were holding back."

"I know," said Daniel. "I know he would. So… you really like it?"

"I do." Ellie smiled.

"Great! D'you see what I've done? The Emporium is so huge, and before it was all so dark and gloomy and… a bit scary to be honest. So I thought, what would make people happy? What would make them comfortable? What sort of place would they want to discover and enjoy? And *then* I thought, well everyone loves a carnival, don't they? So here we are. Every single Wonder in a never-ending city of tents and stalls and rides. Look, over there's the Leap of Faith, the first Wonder I ever saw, remember?"

Ellie laughed at her friend's enthusiasm. "'Course I do!"

"See that one there? With the coloured flags? That's the lion-taming room. And the big gold tent over there? There's a maze inside made of marshmallow. If you get lost you just eat your way out."

Daniel stopped then, fished a golden pocket watch from inside his grey suit jacket. "Blimey, look at the time! We have to open up."

In the very centre of the Carnival of Wonders stood a wrought-iron archway, hung with a familiar pair of rich red velvet curtains. When Daniel and Ellie pushed through them, the sounds and smells of the carnival, the music, the dusky caramel sky all disappeared, and they were standing in the shopfront. This had been the first part of the Nowhere Emporium Daniel had ever encountered, when he'd stumbled in accidentally off the street one day, and the sight of the uncountable number of treasures, the smell of dust, polish and old books, still made him smile, took him back to those exciting early days. The changes he was making inside the Emporium were necessary. The place was too big, too hard to navigate and control, but this was the one part he would never alter. It was perfect.

Daniel walked over to Mr Silver's old desk and opened a drawer. He brought out a book bound in stiff black leather, the title shining up at him in golden letters.

The Wonders of Daniel Holmes

He held the *Book of Wonders* in his hands, fanned

through page after endless page. It still amazed him that this book, this little collection of bound papers, was the key to everything in the Nowhere Emporium. Every room, every Wonder that lay beyond the red curtain, existed only because it had been written in these pages.

"Oi! Wake up!" Ellie was standing over him, her arms folded. "They're waiting." She nodded towards the door, and Daniel stared out through the darkened glass to the gathering crowd outside, people eager to see what lay inside the mysterious shop that had appeared in their town from nowhere.

Daniel placed the *Book of Wonders* in his jacket pocket and nodded to Ellie.

"Where are we today?" she asked.

"Keswick," Daniel replied. "The Lake District. Never been before, but I read in one of Mr Silver's books that they have a cracking little magic district."

In the half a year since Mr Silver's death, Daniel had come to realise that his mentor had only scratched the surface in teaching him about the world of magic. One of the most surprising discoveries Daniel had made, as he travelled through time taking the Emporium from place to place, was that just about every town or city he had visited had a magic district of some description. In some places it was nothing more than a couple of shabby shops, but in others, some of the older towns or larger cities, the magic districts were rambling mazes of streets and alleys crammed with magical stores, houses and museums, all hidden away from the everyday world. Visiting these fascinating places had become Daniel's hobby. But that would have to wait. For now, there was work to do.

Daniel looked to the door, nodded, and fixed the collar of his jacket.

"Showtime."

CHAPTER 2

THE GRAND OPENING

Keswick, Present Day

The people of Keswick had first noticed the shop earlier in the day. It was the strangest thing. Many of the residents of the little town had lived there for their entire lives. They walked past the same shops every day, knew the shopkeepers, knew the streets as well as they knew themselves. And that's what made it impossible.

A new shop had appeared on Main Street.

It had not been there yesterday.

There hadn't even been a shop lying empty that someone had taken over and somehow managed to decorate and stock in the dead of night; that would have been unlikely enough. No, this shop had not opened in place of something else. It had simply appeared, an extra shop in the row.

In a small town like Keswick, word travels fast, and by mid-morning the place was all achatter with whispers of the shop from nowhere.

The Nowhere Emporium.

Shortly after lunch, a sign appeared mysteriously in the window.

GRAND OPENING
—
SUNRISE

And so, next morning when the sun climbed over the edge of the world and the sky turned shades of burning purple and orange, much of the town began to gather outside the shop, muttering and whispering, pointing to the window, trying to see what lay inside.

"I think it's all a big joke," said one.

"I wonder who's inside!" said another.

"What d'you suppose it sells?" said a third.

Then, "Look! Something's happening!"

Something was indeed happening.

The door to the Nowhere Emporium had been guarded by a gated doorway made of shining gold, fine as spun silk. Now, as the sky lightened, the gate crumbled, turned to shimmering dust, and scattered away on the breeze. The crowd gasped and clapped, and when the door to the Emporium opened, they breathed the delicious scents of warm caramel and rich melting chocolate, of old books and starlight.

Someone appeared in the doorway, a boy no more that twelve years old dressed in a smart grey suit, with hair the colour of fire. He stood there for a long, long moment, looked around at the expectant faces as they stared back, hardly knowing what to make of the impossible spectacle.

The boy reached into his pocket, and when he brought out his hand, he was holding what looked like a ball of light, no bigger than a marble, blazing bright. He threw the marble into the air, high into the dawn sky, and it exploded in a shower of dazzling sparks.

The gathered crowd watched, open-mouthed, as the sparks of light multiplied and danced in the air, joined together to make larger, familiar shapes.

"They're birds!" cried a small girl. "Mummy! They're birds!"

The birds were made of light, and they swooped and spun, an entire flock of them, through the dazzled crowd, between legs, over heads, and the people laughed and cheered. Then, as one, the birds darted back up to the sky, spinning around each other, dancing in the air, until the shape of them fell away and they became golden sparks and rained back down to earth.

Silence. The crowd stared at the boy in the doorway, all filled with awe and curiosity. Then he spoke.

"Ladies and gentleman… welcome to the Nowhere Emporium! Inside this shop… *my* shop… you'll find wonders beyond your imagination, a place where anything is possible, a place without limits.

"You won't find anything for sale here besides magic and excitement, and you won't remember any of this tomorrow. But I can promise you that you'll *feel* something is different, that the world will appear sparkling and new. And the price for this, ladies and gentleman? The cost you must pay to fly through the night sky, or feel the wind from a dragon's wings brush your skin? Not money. Not that. No, the price is simple.

"The price of entry is one dream. Dreams are pure imagination, and imagination is the main ingredient of magic. It won't hurt. It won't do you any harm. When you step through the doorway, a dream will fly out of your head and into the Nowhere Emporium, where it will become pure magic, become a part of the place. And in donating your dreams you are making sure that the Emporium will continue to travel, to spread wonder. And the world needs a little wonder, doesn't it?"

A susurration passed through the crowd.

"And now," said the boy, "it's up to you. Come in. Experience the Nowhere Emporium and all of its Wonders." He smiled. "Or don't. The choice is yours."

And with that he turned and disappeared back into the shop, leaving the gathered townsfolk staring at each other, at the entrance to the shop, peering through the window.

"What should we do?"

"Well, I'll tell you one thing – I won't be going in there!"

"I think I'm dreaming. It feels like a dream."

A number of the crowd filtered away. Those people, the ones who didn't enter the Nowhere Emporium, found that when they returned home their memories of the morning were nothing more than empty echoes. They couldn't remember where they had been, or what they had done.

For those who decided to remain, though, the morning was only just beginning.

All it took was one person to enter, one person to take that first step, and the rest would follow. It was always the way.

And so they came.

CHAPTER 3

THE FAN

Keswick, Present Day

Daniel and Ellie stood by the red velvet curtain at the back of the shop, smiling at their customers.

"Glad you could make it," Daniel was saying. "Please come in. Look around. Explore! There's nothing in this place that can hurt you."

He felt eyes on him then, saw that Ellie was staring, a strange smirk on her face.

"What? What is it? Do I have mustard on my nose again?"

She laughed. "No. It's just... you're in danger, Daniel Holmes, of becoming quite good at your job."

Daniel blinked, stared back, feeling the redness spread up his neck.

"You really think so? Really? I think I still *really* need to work on my speech for opening night – I go over the top and scare some of them away and I've never quite got the hang of being mysterious, but that's something I can work on, and then there's the—"

"Daniel! Take a breath before your head explodes! I reckon you're doing just fine. Now, can we please go and get something to eat? I'm starving…"

"Excuse me."

A tall, awkward-looking teenage girl was staring at Daniel quite intensely through large, red-framed spectacles. Her neck was long, her reddish hair wild and bushy. When she caught his eye she smiled, flashing big square front teeth.

"Oh gosh… are you? You *are*, aren't you?"

Daniel looked at Ellie, who shrugged.

"I'm sorry… am I *what?*"

The girl widened her eyes, puffed the air from her cheeks.

"I can't believe I'm *actually* here! I've been waiting so long for you to bring the Nowhere Emporium to Keswick!" She glanced around in a conspiratorial fashion and leaned in, whispering, "I'm from the magic district here. Oh! Can I have a picture with you?"

Daniel shared another puzzled look with Ellie.

"A picture? I'm sorry… why?"

The girl gave him an *I-can't-believe-you-just-asked-me-that* sort of look, her head bobbing excitedly around on the end of her long neck.

"Hel-*lo*! You're Daniel Holmes, the new owner of the Nowhere Emporium! I bet people ask to have their picture with you all the time. Will you do the honours?"

She reached into the flowery canvas bag draped over her bony shoulder and brought out a very large, very old-looking camera, which she bundled into Ellie's hands. Ellie stared at the camera, then at the girl, then at Daniel.

"Um. Right," she said, and grinned. Daniel could almost hear her brain working, and he was not looking forward to the results. "Get nice and close now, Daniel. Put your arm around your new friend, won't you?"

Daniel gingerly put his arm on the girl's shoulder.

"He's got his arm around me!" shrieked the girl as she reached out and grabbed a confused-looking customer by the arm. "Can you believe it? Daniel Holmes has his arm around me! *Me!*"

"That's great." Ellie was clearly enjoying herself. "Come on, Daniel, get closer. I'm sure… I'm sorry, what's your name?"

"Edna Bloom," the girl said with an awkward kind of curtsey, as if she was in the presence of royalty.

"I'm sure Edna won't bite."

Daniel shot Ellie a look which he hoped said, *I'll get you back for this*, then he moved closer to Edna. She smelled like she'd taken a bath in perfume. The camera went off with a blinding flash.

"One more." Ellie flashed a wicked smile. "Daniel, this time why don't you give Edna a little kiss on the cheek?"

Daniel's eyes widened. "Oh. I'm sure she doesn't want that—"

But Edna had already shoved her cheek towards Daniel's lips, and their faces clumsily mashed together just as the flash went off again.

"Perfect." Ellie handed the huge camera back to Edna, who, it seemed, was in danger of exploding.

"Thank you! Oh, thank you!" She grabbed Daniel's hand and shook it with jolting force.

"My... pleasure." He yanked his hand free. "Now, I'm sorry but I must be off. Customers to attend to, you know how it is..."

"Of course," said Edna breathlessly. "Important work to do!" And she gave Daniel another little curtsey as he spun off through the curtain.

As soon as the girl was gone, Ellie melted into a puddle of giggles.

"Well, I'm glad you're having a good time," Daniel huffed, his arms folded tight, his cheeks flushed. They were now in the Emporium proper, away from the shopfront with its jumbled treasures and columns of books, in Daniel's great Carnival of Wonders.

"Come on." Ellie picked herself back up. "You have to admit it was quite funny. A fan. You! I mean, Papa attracted a couple of nutters over the years but… you?"

Daniel's flush deepened. "And why is that so unbelievable?"

"What are you two bickering about?"

The booming voice could only belong to one person: Caleb.

When Ellie's father, Lucien Silver, had been proprietor of the Nowhere Emporium, he had created a small army of characters and used the immense magic of his *Book of Wonders* to bring them to life within the boundaries of the shop. There were clowns and magicians, fire-breathers and acrobats, fortune-tellers and vendors who sold popcorn and toffee apples and hot chocolate pies. Two of these performers, Caleb and Anja, had become very important to Daniel; they were friends and guides, and they had been through so much together that it seemed he had known them forever.

Caleb the fire-breather was a broad giant of a man, and as he strode towards them he seemed to block out most of the twilight sky.

"Daniel has a *fan*," said Ellie, unable to control her delight.

"Ellie, are you going to tell everyone?"

"Of course I am."

Caleb smiled down at Daniel. "A fan? And is this fan... a *girl*?"

"Right," snapped Daniel, "that's enough of that. Get back to work."

Caleb gave a huge, guffawing laugh, bowed, and began to walk away. "Are you coming?" he yelled back at them. "Your newest Wonder has its first customers!"

CHAPTER 4

THE IRON CIRCUS

The Nowhere Emporium, Present Day

"Roll up! Roll up! Roll up to the Iron Circus!"

Many hundreds of people had flocked to the Nowhere Emporium that morning, and upon entering the carnival, a great many of them were now heading for the same Wonder. It was easy to see why. Daniel had only recently put the finishing flourishes to the great Iron Circus, and as he and Ellie approached, nervous tension swirled around his insides.

A great big-top tent rose up higher than any other, all rivets and bolts and sheets of metal bigger than double-decker busses. Atop the tent was a flashing sign welcoming the guests, and many of the Emporium performers had formed a guard of honour at the entrance. As the customers walked between the jugglers and stilt walkers and contortionists, they laughed and gasped and pointed. There was Caleb, breathing fire, the flames from his mouth taking the form of different animals as they blossomed and rolled in the air. And beside him, was Anja, the snake charmer, serpents of many shimmering colours wrapped all around her arms and neck and legs.

Daniel and Ellie waved as they passed through the entrance into the glistening metallic big top, where customers were taking their seats around the main circus ring. When everyone was seated, the lights died away, leaving the huge venue in darkness, save for a single spotlight pointed at the very centre of the ring.

Silence. It was as if every person in the tent was holding their breath. Waiting. Expecting.

Daniel sat forward in his seat as a figure stepped into the light.

The Ringmaster.

But this was no ordinary circus performer. Of course not. This was the Nowhere Emporium, and this was the Iron Circus – one of Daniel Holmes's greatest creations. It would not do for the Ringmaster to be ordinary. He was, like the rest of the circus to which he belonged, made entirely of iron. His iron top hat was studded with rivets. His coat-tails were iron too. His face was made of a great many iron cogs, which spun and switched, rising and falling to create the features of a man. His eyes were round glass lenses, and a warm yellow light glowed behind them as he looked up and around the huge big top at his enrapt audience. His eyes met Daniel's, and the cogs of his face whirred into a smile. Daniel nodded and smiled back.

"He's made of metal!" came one voice from the audience.

"No, he can't be. It's a trick."

Somebody threw a coin, and it spun into the spotlight, hitting the Ringmaster's top hat with a loud clang.

"He is! He's metal!"

The single, booming beat of a drum silenced the audience once more. Then the iron man spoke.

"Welcome," he said in a voice as clear as that of the greatest stage actor, "to the Iron Circus! Many of you may have been to a circus before. Many of you may think you know what to expect here tonight. But I promise: you have never seen anything quite like this. Your senses will be dazzled. Your mind will be set ablaze. Are you ready?"

"Yes," came a murmured whisper from the crowd.

"Then let the show begin!"

The lights came up, and the Iron Circus filled with colourful fireworks and smoke. When the smoke had cleared, the Ringmaster was gone, and the circus ring was filled instead with dancing iron elephants, duelling iron knights and iron trapeze artists soaring high above. Each act made the crowd stand and cheer and whoop.

Somewhere in the audience, Edna Bloom – Daniel's greatest fan – raised her old camera and the flashbulb blazed again and again as she took photographs of each wondrous act, her heart filling with happiness.

She was just about to take what would have been a marvellous snap of one of the iron trapeze artists mid-flight when her finger paused on the button. The roar of the crowd suddenly seemed to die away, becoming echoing and distant, though when Edna looked around she could see that they were still cheering as loudly as ever. She stuck a finger in her ear and twisted it, wondering if there was something wrong with her hearing.

The world seemed to slow down around her.

"Edna."

The voice was loud and clear.

"Who's that? What's happening?" She looked around at the crowd, all moving strangely slowly, the wide-eyed, cheering expressions frozen comically on their faces.

"Edna."

There was something about that voice she

recognised, something warm and comforting, something that drew her in... She stood up and filed out of the row, down the steps, and out of the Iron Circus.

"Edna."

"Where are you?" she called out.

"Come to me, Edna. I'm waiting."

The voice was hard to resist. So Edna began to walk, through the city of tents, towards it.

CHAPTER 5

A VANISHING

The Nowhere Emporium, Present Day

"I think it's safe to say this carnival of yours is a hit," said Ellie.

"Really?" Daniel sounded a little unsure.

"Daniel, are you kidding? Seriously? You didn't see how happy those people were?"

"Yeah… I mean I did, but…"

"But nothing." Ellie bumped his shoulder encouragingly. "Just be happy about it. I heard one boy telling his mum this was the best day of his life."

"Really?"

"You bet. He'd just come out of that Wonder you

made a few weeks ago – you know, the one where you can fight giant robots against each other?"

"That is a good one." Daniel stroked his chin.

It was early afternoon, and the Emporium had gathered more than enough dreams from its customers to refuel. Daniel had decided to close up early, and he and Ellie were walking from tent to tent, making sure all the customers knew it was time to leave.

"Can't I just do one more?" pleaded the last of the stragglers, a man in his mid-seventies who was hopping around like a schoolboy who had eaten too many sweets. "Please?"

"I'm sorry to be a spoilsport, sir," said Daniel, "but rules are rules. This way, please. That's right, towards the archway there, and through the curtain."

The old man made his way towards the exit, shoulders slumped.

"Surely everyone's accounted for now?" said Ellie when the man had gone.

Daniel concentrated, half-closing his eyes. He could feel the Emporium, everything in it, every Wonder, every performer and vendor and guest.

"There's still someone else."

Ellie shook her head indignantly. "We made the closing announcement half an hour ago. That's just rude!"

"I'll make another one." Daniel strode over to Mr Silver's desk. (*No*, he thought... *MY desk. I have to start thinking of it as mine.*) He was surprised to feel a sense of unease slowly creeping over him. Standing on his desk was an old-fashioned microphone – another of Daniel's additions – and when he picked it up and held it to his mouth, a piercing howl of feedback made Ellie stick her fingers in her ears.

"Oops, sorry. There. That's better. Hem hem. Ladies and gentlemen, this is a FINAL call to remind you that the Nowhere Emporium is now closed. Please make your way *IMMEDIATELY* to the red-curtained exit archway at the centre of the carnival. If you fail to exit the store, I'm afraid I will have no choice but to send a hungry troll to escort you off the premises. Thank you."

Ellie raised an eyebrow. "A troll?"

Daniel shrugged. "Well, I had to make it sound a wee bit scary, didn't I?"

Somewhere in the Carnival of Wonders, Edna Bloom heard Daniel's voice echoing through the toffee-apple-infused air, but she did not head for the exit as instructed.

"Don't bother with him," said the voice she was chasing, the somehow familiar voice that had sought her out in the Iron Circus. "I'm waiting…"

How many miles have I walked? Edna wondered, glancing back over her shoulder. Tents of every description stretched off into the distance. The Nowhere Emporium was so wonderful – more incredible than even her wild imagination had allowed her to believe – and her search for the owner of this mysterious voice had taken her into many of the Wonders. In one tent she had walked with dinosaurs. In another she had been transported to a beautiful coral reef in an ocean the colour of sapphires.

Edna came to a stop, because there was a small tent blocking the way ahead. It was made of black canvas and she was positive that it had not been there only a moment ago. The entranceway was rippling as if someone had just gone through.

"Edna. Come on, Edna." The voice drifted from the tent, and as Edna took a faltering step towards it, she thought that it sounded just like…

Grandpa!

He'd been the first to tell her of the Nowhere Emporium. He'd owned a shop in Keswick's magic district, selling potion ingredients that he'd picked in the woods himself. Sometimes Edna would join him.

"It's the greatest piece of magic in the world," he'd once told her. "There are so many Wonders, you could walk around your entire life and never see them all. Not even close."

"Have you been, Grandpa? Have you seen it for yourself?"

The old man had picked a bunch of fresh garlic from the woodland floor, smelled it, and smiled.

"Only once. A long time ago."

Edna's eyes had widened. "What did you see?"

"Magic unlike anything I'd seen before, or have come across since. Rooms filled with waterfalls and towns made of marzipan. And another where I could see music – actually see it in the air, blooming like crystal flowers!"

"What else? What else, Grandpa?"

"I met the owner," he'd said. "Shook his hand. I've never felt so much power in all my life. The magic was crackling through him."

Ever since that day, Edna had been hooked. She'd tried to find out about the Emporium, but information had been sparse. The snippets she had managed to find, in old books or newspapers, had been vague. And then, all of a sudden, half a year back, everything had changed and the Nowhere Emporium was suddenly everywhere, in magical newspapers and magazines. There was a new owner, Daniel Holmes, and it seemed he didn't feel the need to hide away in the same way Lucien Silver had done.

And now, here she was, hardly able to believe that the Nowhere Emporium had come to her town, that she was experiencing its Wonders for herself.

She wished her grandpa could have been with her. "Edna."

Her heart was a hammer in her ears. That voice. Could it be?

She took a step forward, and another, and another, until she stood only a foot from the tent entrance. She peered into the darkness, tried to make out something, anything, but it was impenetrable.

"Come on in, Edna," said the voice again. She felt it wrapping around her, and she shivered.

For the first time there was a niggle of doubt in her mind. She took a slow step back.

The voice pushed once more. "Come on in, Eddy. It's safe and warm in here."

Eddy. Only Grandpa had ever called her that. Her niggling doubt vanished, replaced by impossible joy.

"G-grandpa?"

"That's right, Eddy. It's me. Oh, you should see it in here!"

How she had missed that old voice! Recently when she'd thought of him she had struggled to picture his face or remember what he sounded like, and she was worried that she was beginning to forget him.

"What's in there, Grandpa?" Edna peered through the dark entrance, hoping to catch a glimpse of his smiling face.

"Oh, it's beautiful, Eddy. You'd love it. Come on through. I can't come out there."

Edna brushed through the entrance, into the tent.

Inside was a small, bare space. The floor was dry grass, and in the centre stood a tall mirror framed with dark wood. As Edna approached the mirror, she saw her reflection, saw the puzzled look on her own face. But she also saw something else, something behind the surface of the glass: a dark, smoky shape drifting lazily.

She moved closer, until she was near enough to reach out and touch the mirror. Behind the glass, the smoke swirled and formed the shape of a man, who stepped forward so that she could see him.

Edna felt her breath choke in her throat. Her head spun and her eyes burned with tears.

"Grandpa!"

There was the old man, just as she remembered him, with his thinning grey hair, wild eyebrows and ears that were two sizes too big for his head. He smiled out sadly at her, and he placed his hand on the other side of the mirror. Edna reached out, tried to put her hand on his, but the glass separated them.

"Help me, Eddy," he said. "I'm stuck in here. I want to get out. I want to be with you."

Edna swallowed and nodded. "I'll help you. I'll get you out."

She looked around, but there was nothing she could use to break the glass. Then her fingers brushed the camera around her neck, and her eyes widened.

She grasped the camera tight, reared back and brought it down hard against the mirror.

The glass did not break. Edna's camera broke instead, fragments of it falling to the dry grass.

"Not that way," Grandpa told her. "Magic. It has to be magic, Eddy."

She fumbled around in her coat, pulled out her spell book. She had been studying hard and she was getting good. Flicking to the correct page, she reached out and placed one finger on the glass, and recited the spell from the pages of her book. As she spoke, she felt the tip of her finger heating up, becoming so hot that she worried it might burst into flames. Cracks began to appear on the surface of the mirror, first at the place where her finger touched the glass and then spreading out in a ripple, until the entire mirror was frosted with them.

Edna read the last word of the spell, and the glass shattered and fell to the grass. She shook her hand, tried to cool the tip of her finger, which was now smoking.

"I did it! Grandpa, you can come out."

Where the surface of the mirror had been, there was now a doorway into thick darkness. Slowly, from the pitch black, an arm reached out. There was something off about the arm. Perhaps it was too long, or maybe it was the way the fingers moved and twitched.

Edna stared at it.

The hand opened, beckoned her with a finger.

"It's only me," said the voice of her grandpa. "You're safe here."

Her heart ached to see him, to hug him and speak to him.

She reached out.

The hand clamped around her wrist, and before she could scream, it dragged her into the darkness.

CHAPTER 6

FORK IN THE ROAD

The Nowhere Emporium, Present Day

"What are we looking for, Daniel?"

"I'm not sure. Something bad…"

Daniel was moving so quickly that Ellie could barely keep up, through the alleyways between tents and stalls, further and further from the shopfront, until he skidded to a stop, and pointed.

"That. That's it."

"What?" asked Ellie. "That little black tent? You sure?"

Daniel brought out the *Book of Wonders*, flicked through the pages.

"I remember this… When I first took over and

I was repairing all the damage to the Emporium, I found this. Look."

He held out the book at the open page and Ellie read the message written there.

The mirror
Danger. Failed experiment.
Strictly not for public consumption.
Keep hidden.

"That's Papa's writing…"

"Yeah," said Daniel. "I tried to get rid of the tent for good, but it wouldn't go, so I kept it hidden deep inside the Emporium. Come on…"

They entered the tent, and there, on the dry grass, stood a tall mirror. There seemed nothing unusual at all about the mirror; its surface was smooth and shining and perfect, and there was nothing else in the tent.

"What's dangerous about this?" said Ellie.

Daniel shrugged. "I dunno. But there must be something, otherwise why would your dad have kept it hidden? I mean, how come it's just appeared in my carnival?" He paused, and bent down, picking up a piece of dark plastic from the grass. "Someone's been in here."

"You know what's happened, don't you?" said Ellie.

"One of your customers found this Wonder, came in and got some sort of fright. I dunno, maybe they saw a ghost in the mirror or something. Then they snuck out while we were on the way here."

Daniel stared at the mirror.

"Maybe. Something just doesn't feel right, Ellie."

She shook her head. "You're starting to sound like Papa. This place is getting under your skin, making you paranoid. Not every bad feeling you have means a disaster is around the corner, Daniel. Just hide this tent again and forget about it."

"You're right," said Daniel. "I have been working a bit too much. Maybe I need a break."

Ellie smiled. "Now you're talking!"

They left the tent, and Daniel scribbled something in the *Book of Wonders*. Just like that, the black canvas tent was gone, hidden away again, deep inside the Emporium.

"Feel better?" Ellie asked.

"A wee bit." Daniel smiled, tapped the book. "I almost forgot. I've made you a surprise. Come on."

Deep inside the Emporium, in the black canvas tent, the surface of the mirror cracked and shattered and fell to the ground once more. Where the glass had been, the dark doorway reappeared, and from it stepped

Edna Bloom. To her, it felt almost like a dream as she left the tent and began making her way through the Carnival of Wonders. She couldn't remember exactly what had happened, only that there had been... a mirror? And a voice?

When she looked back, the black tent was gone.

Edna looked around, feeling strangely dazed. She sniffed the air, smelling the saccharine scents of candyfloss and ice cream. She came to a fork in the path.

A sign on the first path read:

A sign on the second path read:

She took a step towards the EXIT path, but then she stopped. There was a peculiar feeling gnawing away at her insides like a worm in an apple.

I'm supposed to find something. Something important. But what?

She thought she saw movement from the corner

of her eye, and she spun around, but the only thing there was her shadow.

Edna turned back to the sign. She knew that she should go home, that if she didn't her mum would go mad with worry. But every time these thoughts entered her head, they would turn to dust in the blazing heat of another thought.

Find it. Find the Fountain.

She couldn't resist. She chose her path and walked towards OTHER THINGS.

CHAPTER 7

A PICNIC ON THE MOON

The Nowhere Emporium, Present Day

The new tent was made of shimmering material in such a dark blue that it almost seemed black, and dappled with hundreds, or even thousands of golden stars that twinkled in the twilight.

"What is it?" Ellie asked, stroking the soft material.

"If I told you it wouldn't be a surprise, would it?"

"But you've never made me a surprise before."

"Then it's the perfect time, isn't it? Are you going in or what?"

She examined the entranceway, reached for the curtains, then stopped and fixed Daniel with an appraising look.

"This better not be a trick, Daniel Holmes. If I walk through here and get ambushed by… by mud pixies or something, I swear it'll be the last Wonder you ever write."

He smirked.

"Mud pixies? That's actually not bad. I'll have to remember that."

She made to punch him on the arm, but he dodged her hand.

"Relax! It's not anything bad, I promise. Just go in!"

Ellie took two fingers and pointed at her own eyes, then at Daniel's – the classic 'I'm watching you' gesture. Then she cautiously made her way through the curtain and into the sparkling tent.

Daniel gave her a few moments alone. Then he took the *Book of Wonders*, tucked it into the inside pocket of his suit jacket, gave it a pat, and followed her through.

Ellie stood just on the other side of the curtain. Daniel joined her, but she didn't turn to look at him; she simply continued to stare in quiet wonder at her surroundings. The surface of the scene in front of her was dry and rocky and colourless, mostly flat to the horizon in all directions, save for an unimaginable number of craters. Large craters, small craters, craters within craters within craters. Beyond that, an infinite expanse of black sky spread out forever, glittering and shimmering with more stars than there were numbers to count them. And hanging in that blackness, the Earth: a glowing blue marble half-lit by the golden warmth of the distant Sun.

"It's… amazing," whispered Ellie. "It's wonderful… It's…"

"Yours," finished Daniel.

"What?'"

Daniel turned to face her. "I can't imagine what you've been going through since your dad died, Ellie. He's been gone six months, but everywhere you look you must see him, reminders of him, things he created. And you haven't complained once. Not a single time. I'm just starting to feel comfortable as owner of the Emporium now, and a big part of that is down to you. Helping me. Guiding me. Not hating me for taking over from Mr Silver."

He could see her eyes were brimming with tears, see the sparkle of them in the half-light.

"We have all of this," he went on, "so many Wonders, but none of it really belongs to you. I want you to have a place where you can come, a place that's yours and nobody else's. A place where you can think, or cry, or scream and nobody else will ever know. And if you want to be alone, what better place than the Moon, eh? So, here it is."

Ellie made a sort of muffled choking sound, and then smacked him on the arm.

"Aaoow!"

Then she hugged him.

"Thank you," she murmured.

Daniel was so shocked by her reaction that he wasn't quite sure what to do. "Um. Are you hungry?"

Ellie broke away and wiped her eyes, and they stood a little awkwardly, the Earth rising majestically among the stars behind them.

"Yeah, actually." She sniffed. "I am."

Daniel took out the *Book of Wonders*, opened it and scribbled something down. Then he closed the book and stowed it away in his pocket once more. He looked behind Ellie and smiled at what he saw. He motioned for her to turn around.

On the cratered ground there was a red blanket, and on the blanket a collection of plates filled with delicious-looking food: roast beef sandwiches, sausage rolls, crusty bread spread thickly with butter, pancakes, custard tarts, jugs of iced lemonade.

It was every bit as tasty as it looked, all of it, and they sat and happily munched under the stars until Daniel noticed that Ellie had become quiet and was staring down at the Earth with a faraway expression.

"You OK?" he asked.

"Hmm? Oh. Yeah." She tilted her head to one side, nodded towards Earth. "It seems such a big place when you're down there, doesn't it. You don't imagine anything could ever happen to it. But from out here you realise how small and fragile it really is. How many people do you reckon live down there?"

"I dunno." Daniel shrugged. "Seven billion. Ish."

"Seven billion people. Do you know, Daniel, I've never had a friend outside the Emporium?"

"You meet loads of people. We both do."

"That's true. We meet them. We say hello as they pass through, and then we move on. But we don't *know* anyone. Everyone has a story, Daniel. Every single one of the seven billion down there. I want to hear some of them. And I want to write my own."

Daniel gave her a sideways look. "What are you getting at, Ellie?"

She continued to gaze down at the Earth and then seemed to shake herself awake.

"Don't mind me." She picked up an apple, shining it on her sweater. "I'm tired is all. I love this place. Thank you for making it for me, Daniel."

And there they sat for a while, eating and drinking as the Earth spun among the stars.

CHAPTER 8

THE VISITOR

London, 1967

Valerie Mildew sat up in bed, a haze of dream and sleep swirling around her. When the mist had lifted and her head was clear, she reached over, her old muscles protesting, and switched on the lamp on the bedside table. She looked at the clock: two in the morning.

Valerie swung her legs round and sat on the edge of the bed, her feet searching for her slippers. She stood up, creaking and popping and groaning, and stretched the stiffness out of her back. Her gaze lingered first upon the photograph on the bedside table, the one showing Valerie and her dear husband many years ago, and then on the empty side of the bed, the place where he used to sleep.

Valerie shuffled out of her bedroom and downstairs to the kitchen, where she boiled the kettle and made herself a good strong cup of tea and cut a large slice from the walnut cake she'd baked yesterday. The night was calm and silent, and Valerie sat alone in her kitchen. She ate her cake and sipped her tea, until the plate was cleared and the cup was empty. After that, Valerie went to the lounge. She sat down at her old piano and began to play.

Her old fingers were knotted and twisted, so she couldn't play as beautifully as she once had. But still, most of the notes were correct. When her fingers grew tired, she rested them in her lap, but the music continued, the keys of the piano rising and falling all on their own. As Valerie listened, a smile lit up her wrinkled face, made her look younger, *feel* younger. At last she stopped the music. She closed the lid of the piano and turned around. Her eyes searched the lounge.

"I know you're here," she said. "I can feel you. You've been watching me. Why don't you come out and face me, eh?"

Something strange happened to an empty patch of air across the room, and Valerie realised that it was not an empty patch of air at all; there was something there, so clear it was almost invisible... but if you looked carefully enough, you could see the light bending around it, distorting, the way it does when it travels through glass.

Valerie stood up, took a small step towards the shape.

"Whoever you are... *whatever* you are, I only ask that you make this quick. I couldn't put up a fight even if I wanted to, which I don't by the way. I'm old. I'm tired. I'm ready."

Across the room, the light bent around the strange creature, warped as it passed through. There were hints, in certain places, of familiar glassy shapes catching the light: a hand, a foot... a face.

Valerie took a step back, let out a sharp breath.

"You", she whispered. "But it *can't* be you..."

What might have been a hand rose up and pointed a finger, and Valerie's eyes were drawn to her own shadow on the worn carpet, which had begun to move, to change shape, to rise up from the ground and loom over her. Valerie cowered, stumbled back, and as her shadow swallowed her up, she gave a single final scream.

Next day, at around eleven in the morning, a black Rolls Royce Phantom drove smoothly around the corner and pulled up outside Valerie's house.

The driver killed the engine. "This the place, Mr Ivy, sir?"

Mr Ivy lowered the darkened passenger window. He nodded.

"Yes, Kenworth. Thank you. Wait here, please." And he climbed out.

The rear doors opened, and out stepped Mrs Hennypeck and Flintwitch.

Mr Ivy adjusted the crimson scarf around his neck and surveyed the quiet street. Curtains twitched in the windows of neighbouring houses. He rang the doorbell.

Through the frosted glass of the front door they saw someone approaching. When it opened they were met with the pale, worried face of a smartly dressed woman in her sixties.

Mr Ivy reached into his coat, brought out a wallet and opened it, showing the woman a badge with a photograph of himself. Under the photograph, in silver letters were the words:

Abraham Ivy
Chief Investigator
Bureau of Magical Investigation

The woman in the doorway nodded. "Thank goodness. I've never had to call your Bureau before. I wasn't sure my message would get there. I'm Ada Mildew. This is…" She brushed the hair from her face distractedly. "This is my mother's house. Please, come in. I think something terrible has happened to her."

"We're here to help, Ada," said Mr Ivy calmly. "Please, show us what you've found."

Ada led them into the house, which smelled flowery, like springtime, and along the hallway to a large, bright lounge. There were comfortable-looking couches and a piano and a smattering of ornaments – all of which looked like they belonged in the house of an elderly woman. But there was something else. Something that most definitely did not belong.

"There," said Ada Mildew, her voice wavering slightly. "There it is." She nodded at the carpet a little way across the room.

Mr Ivy and the others approached carefully.

On the floor was a shadow. But this shadow hadn't been cast by anything in the room, not the furniture or the people present. This was the shadow of someone who was no longer there.

"It's Mum," said Ada. She was shaking badly and her eyes glistened. "I know it's her."

Mr Ivy nodded to young Flintwitch.

"Oh," said Flintwitch. "Right. Er, why don't you come with me, Ms Mildew? I'll get you a cup of tea."

Ada looked down at him.

"Oh my. You're just a nipper, aren't you?"

"Nipper?" Flintwitch looked scandalised.

"I assure you Flintwitch makes a splendid cup of tea." Mr Ivy smiled reassuringly, and Ada led Flintwitch towards the kitchen. Before he disappeared, he gave Mr Ivy a look which clearly said: *Why do I always have to make the tea?*

Mr Ivy shared a knowing look with Mrs Hennypeck. They crouched over the strange abandoned shadow on the floor, examined it closely.

"Another one," said Mrs Hennypeck. She may have been dead, her skin cold and blue-tinged, but her eyes were very much alive, and filled now with sadness. "Valerie was one of the good ones."

"When did you see her last?" asked Mr Ivy.

"Oh, I haven't seen Valerie since she left the Bureau. That must be... what, fifty years ago?"

Mr Ivy nodded towards the door. "Do you think the daughter knows about her mother's past?"

Mrs Hennypeck shook her head. "No. Valerie left the Bureau because she wanted away from all of it. She wanted to start a family, and you can't really do that when you spend all hours of the day and night chasing magical criminals."

Mr Ivy stood up and straightened his suit. He stared down at the strange shadow and wondered what exactly had happened to the woman who once cast it. Whatever it was, it could not be good.

"Four investigators. All long retired. All made to disappear. Why?"

"That's the question," said Mrs Hennypeck. "And if we don't answer it soon, I'm afraid things will only get worse. I have a terrible feeling about this, Mr Ivy."

Mr Ivy went to the wide window and stared out into the street.

"Unfortunately, Mrs Hennypeck, I'm inclined to agree."

CHAPTER 9

WITHOUT A TRACE

Keswick, Present Day

"Hello? Is anyone here?"

Edna Bloom pushed through the red velvet curtain, into the shopfront of the Nowhere Emporium. She had been walking for what felt like days. She was ravenous, and there was an ache in her head and a feeling of unease bubbling away in the pit of her stomach.

The shopfront was silent, deserted. She spotted a half-eaten sandwich lying on Daniel Holmes's desk, and she dashed over and stuffed it into her mouth, her eyes closing as she chewed.

Why am I even still here? she thought. She

examined the camera around her neck, the jagged places where pieces had broken off, and she couldn't remember how it had been damaged. *The Fountain. I was looking for something called the Fountain. But why? I've never even heard of it before.*

It was as if the mist was beginning to lift from her brain, and she was thinking clearly for the first time in ages. This place was doing strange things to her. Maybe she didn't like it here so much after all. She thought of her mum, out there, worried sick…

Edna moved to the front door of the shop. Through the window she could see the busy weekend market in Keswick's Main Street, hear the rabble of voices and laughter and barking dogs.

She reached for the door handle.

Tried to reach for the door handle.

Her arm didn't move.

"What the—?"

She tried again, but it was as if her body belonged to someone else.

And then, in the corner of her vision, she saw movement on the floor. She looked down and took a sharp breath. She was sure she had seen her shadow moving on its own. But that was mad, wasn't it?

"The Fountain," she said to herself. "Need more time to find the Fountain."

It was as if these thoughts were being planted in her head, that they belonged to someone else.

Edna found herself moving, walking to a curious instrument on the wall with many dials and hands, and knowing, somehow, that she should turn these dials to precise points.

Another quarter turn there. Three more clicks for that one. Good. But how do I know that? What am I doing?

Next, she moved to the fireplace, reached into the bucket, picked up a handful of coal, and tossed it in the fire. As the coal hit the fire, the flames licked higher, shifted through many changes of colour, until they burned red. The Nowhere Emporium lurched. Then a cloud of soot exploded from the fireplace. When the dust had settled, Edna could no longer hear the sounds of the street market, of the crowds. And she knew she was no longer in Keswick.

"Daniel, come on! I'm shattered!"

"OK, OK!"

Keswick's magic district was one of the oldest in Britain, a single winding lane off the main street, hidden from non-magic folk by powerful enchantments. Daniel had been wandering around taking photos of the old buildings, and he wished he could split himself up into pieces so he could visit all the stores at once.

"Get your crab apples here!" yelled a lady from a stall. In front of her was a basket filled with green apples, but they had snapping, grabbing little claws like crabs, and they kept trying to escape.

"No-stink socks!" yelled another trader. "Wear the same socks every day without so much as a whiff!"

"Part-used cauldrons!"

"Dragon scales!"

They had already been to an apothecary, where Daniel bought some ingredients including pixie root and exploding moon weed. He was beginning to try his hand at potion-making, but he didn't seem to have the knack; on his last attempt he'd tried to mix up a serum that would make him taller, but instead had caused him to grow a magnificent ginger moustache. He'd had to travel to New England to have a witch specialising in magical mishaps remove it. He also bought a new suit from The Witch's Closet and a comic from Scattergood's News and Tobacco –

SELF-FILLING PIPES NOW IN STOCK!

As they wound along the alley they passed a magical pet shop where a shopkeeper was wrestling with what looked like a fur-covered lizard, and a toy shop where a great many tiny metal soldiers were in the midst of a battle in the window display, miniature cannons firing, horses galloping and muskets smoking.

They walked around a ladder set against a leaning clock tower. Atop the ladder was a man in overalls holding a long stick with a glowing blue tip, which he was using to poke at a huge creature that looked like a cross between a bat and an eagle. It had great leathery wings, a body covered in black feathers and an enormously long beak filled with sharp teeth, and it was hanging upside down in the darkness of the belfry. The man muttered, "Clear off you stupid great overgrown bag of feathers!"

"That bloke's either really brave or really crazy," said Ellie. "A moonghast'll take your arm right off!"

Through the street they went, out of the magic district to Keswick's Main Street, past the picturesque town hall and the old hotels and shops. The weekend market was up and running, selling the everyday folk flowers and cheese and meat and clothes and ornaments, and food stalls filled the cool autumn air with the aroma of frying onions and hot sugary donuts.

Pushing through the crowd, Daniel and Ellie reached the other side of the pedestrianised street, where they stopped and stared.

For several moments – it seemed to Daniel like a terribly long time – neither of them spoke. Daniel *could not* speak, because the lump of panic lodged in his throat was choking him.

"Daniel?" Ellie's voice rose questioningly.

"Yeah?" He gulped.

"Where's the Emporium?"

Daniel did not answer, because he did not know how to. They were staring at the spot where the Emporium should be, the spot they'd left it less than an hour ago, right next to the famous Keswick Chocolate Shop. Only now there was no golden sign or midnight-coloured brick, no trace of the familiar archway.

The Nowhere Emporium was gone.

CHAPTER 10

THE SEARCH BEGINS

Keswick, Present Day

"What did you do?"

"Nothing!"

"How can you lose a shop? *A shop*, Daniel! I mean, people lose wallets and coins and socks. But a shop! It's not like it can fall down the back of the couch, is it?"

Daniel was still staring at the place on Keswick Main Street where the Nowhere Emporium had been only a few hours ago. He was replaying everything in his mind: closing up the shop, making sure the door was locked…

"I didn't do anything different," he said. "I locked the door. I swear!"

Wave after wave of sickness and panic crashed over him. It felt like someone had pulled the plug on the bottom of his world and he was being sucked down, into darkness. He sank down onto the kerb.

Ellie was pacing back and forth on the pavement, causing shoppers to swerve around her.

Suddenly she stopped, almost stepping on a passing sausage dog, and held up a finger.

"The book! The *Book of Wonders!*"

A flash of hope. Daniel reached into his coat, pulled out the black leather book and opened it. Before he'd passed away, Lucien Silver had left an echo of his knowledge in the pages. Daniel had spoken to the echo numerous times; it was a strange experience, because it was like talking to fragments of Mr Silver's personality, like looking at him in a cracked mirror.

"Mr Silver," he said. "Mr Silver! We need your help!" He felt eyes on him, and realised that people walking past were giving him funny looks. The book sat silent and still in his hands. Not so much as a single page rustled. The spark of hope fizzled out. "It's not going to work, Ellie. The book won't work outside the shop."

"Maybe the Emporium just moved," Ellie said hopefully, "to another street?"

Daniel shook his head. "No. It's gone. I can feel it."

And it was true: Daniel could feel that the shop was far away, just as surely as he would feel it if he woke up one morning missing an arm. The Emporium was part of him now, and he a part of it.

It was then that he let the panic take hold of him. He found it difficult to breathe. What would Mr Silver have thought of this? *Good job, Danny boy! You've only gone and misplaced the greatest piece of magic of modern times! Three cheers!*

Ellie must have noticed the manic look on his face, because her own expression softened. "Are you OK?"

"No, Ellie, I'm not OK. I am very much *not* OK. The Emporium is gone! And I don't have the faintest bloomin' clue whether it picked up and decided to leave on its own, or if I messed up somehow, or even if it's been stolen!"

She sat next to him on the pavement. "What are we going to do?"

Daniel stared at the paving stones and at the feet of the passers-by. Troubled thoughts gathered in his mind like storm clouds.

"Ellie, you don't think there's a chance… this can't be Sharpe, can it?"

She looked at him like he was growing another nose. "Daniel, we took care of him. He's gone."

Daniel nodded, but he wasn't so sure. Vindictus Sharpe had been an enemy of Ellie's father. He'd come close to destroying the Emporium for good and stealing the *Book of Wonders*. Thankfully, Daniel had outsmarted Sharpe, erased one of the rooms from the Emporium while he was inside. But what did that really mean? Was he gone forever? Or was part of him still in there, scratching around? Daniel's mind was running away now. He pictured Sharpe creeping around the Emporium's dark places, watching, waiting.

"Hey, Daniel." Ellie jolted him out of his bleak imaginings.

"Mmm?"

She had wrapped a lock of her hair around a finger, and was twirling it in a thoughtful sort of way. "Speaking of Sharpe, you ever wondered how he found the Emporium?"

"How d'you mean?"

"Well, we know Papa was running away from him for a long time, right? We know Sharpe was chasing. But how did he know where to look?"

Daniel stared at her, his mind lighting up. "You're right!"

"Course I'm right! I'm me."

"He must have had some way of tracking the shop," said Daniel. "And if he could do it…"

"So can we!" Ellie finished his thought. Then she added, "Maybe."

They jumped up, startling a couple of pigeons pecking the ground by their shoes, and ran back through the crowds towards the enchanted entrance to Keswick's magic district.

CHAPTER 11

A HOPEFUL LEAD

Keswick, Present Day

The early evening autumn sun was low by the time they had searched the magic district and found Folio and Son's Bookshop, the sky brushed with strokes of burning crimson. A welcoming glow spilled from the window, and they were thankful for the fire's warmth when they walked through the door.

Now, bookshops are magical places at the best of times, filled with words and possibilities and uncountable adventures, but a truly magical bookshop is something else. Folio and Son's was a dimly lit maze of bookshelves, the air thick with dust and the smell of bound paper. A number of the books themselves seemed to be alive, and they flapped, bird-like, across the store from shelf to shelf.

Behind the counter, the shopkeeper was hunched over, doing his best to repair the binding of a small red book, which was trying madly to get away from him. Daniel and Ellie approached him, but Daniel had only just opened his mouth to speak when the shop door suddenly burst open and in hurried a very agitated-looking woman. She pushed past to the counter, and the shopkeeper looked up from his half-repaired book.

"Crikey, Beth! Are you OK?"

The woman, Beth, looked desperately around the place.

"Mort, have you seen my Edna?"

The shopkeeper stuffed the half-repaired book, thrashing and snapping, into a drawer. He stepped out from behind his counter.

"Now, just calm down, Beth. Breathe. What's this about Edna?"

"She hasn't come home," said the woman. "It's not like her at all. I thought she might be in here?"

"I'm sorry, Beth," the shopkeeper said. "I haven't seen her at all today."

The woman's face crumpled. "It's not like her to go off and not tell me. Not like her at all. Oh, Mort, if something's happened to her…"

The shopkeeper shook his head. "Now, I know

you're worried but you mustn't let your imagination get away with you. I'm sure there's a perfectly fine reason why she hasn't come home. I wonder if she hasn't gone down to the lake with some of the other kids? The chestnut trees down there are ripe for the picking."

The woman shook her head in a distracted way, as if the question was an insect buzzing about her face.

"You know the other kids won't let her join in, Mort. My Edna doesn't fit in with them – that's why she spends most of her Saturdays in here with her nose in a spell book."

Suddenly Daniel's eyes shot wide open. He elbowed Ellie, and she turned and made to elbow him back, then saw the look on his face.

"What is it?"

"Edna," he whispered. "The girl who came to the shop. You took our photo, remember?"

Ellie nodded, and her own eyes widened. "She's missing? You don't think… when you felt someone was still in the shop… it wasn't her?"

Daniel chewed on his lip. "But why would she take the Emporium? And how?"

"Should we tell her mum?"

Daniel shook his head. "No. Not yet. We don't even know if Edna has anything to do with this. We'll find the Emporium first, and sort everything out from there."

At the counter, Edna's mum was still in conversation

with the shopkeeper. "You want me to help?" he was asking. "I could shut up shop early and come with you?"

"Oh, no, Mort. There's no need for that. No, it'll be fine." She wrung her hands together. "I'm sure there's a simple explanation, like you said. I wonder if she hasn't gone for a walk in the woods. She used to walk there with her grandfather, you remember?" She hurried to the door, and the shopkeeper held it open.

"You let me know when you find her," he called after her. "And, Beth, if you need any help just say the word."

The door swung shut on the darkening autumn afternoon, and the shopkeeper turned to Daniel and Ellie. There was a flash of recognition in his eyes. "I know you. You're Daniel Holmes."

Daniel felt his cheeks flush. When he'd taken over the Nowhere Emporium one of the first things he did was to let everyone in the magical world know that they were welcome. Lucien Silver had locked the doors and shut himself away, which led to whispers and rumours; Daniel had been quite startled to find that at first everyone he met in the magic districts seemed to be frightened of him

Things were slowly improving, but something unexpected had happened along the way, something Daniel had never bargained for – his name had become somewhat famous. People the world over were beginning to chatter about the shop of wonder, the most marvellous piece of magic they'd ever seen.

Magical newspapers had run reviews and articles. Today, when Edna came to the Emporium, had been the first time he'd met an actual fan, and he wasn't sure that he liked it.

"I heard you'd arrived," said Mort, the shopkeeper. "Was planning on paying you a visit tomorrow, hoping to see what all the fuss is about. Will you still be in town then?"

"Oh, I don't think we'll be going anywhere,'" said Ellie, with a sideways glance at Daniel.

"Great! Oh, I'm sorry, where are my manners? Quite forgot myself. What can I do for you? My shop's not quite as grand as yours, I imagine, but we have a fair collection…"

"It's brilliant," said Daniel. "Really brilliant."

"He's a bookworm," said Ellie.

Mort smiled, wide and warm and genuine, and he cupped his hand to his mouth and whispered, "All the best people are!"

"We were actually hoping you could help us with a spell," Daniel said.

The shopkeeper raised his eyebrows. "Me? Well… I'm not a great magician by any stretch. I'm not bad at simple stuff, but… well, I'm sure you're much more capable."

"Actually, I'm still only learning. I'm fine in the Emporium, but outside I don't really have any experience."

"And I'm no good at this sort of thing," added Ellie. "Seriously, I'm about as magically gifted as a potato."

The shopkeeper frowned. "I see. What sort of spell are you looking to cast?"

"We've lost something," Daniel told him. "And we want to find it again."

Mort held up a finger. "Ah! I might just be able to help you there!" He turned and began skimming his bookshelves, running a finger along the spines of the many books as he went up and down the rows. "Here we are." He clicked his fingers, and one of the books on the highest shelf flapped down and landed in his outstretched hands. "*Pickwick and Pickwick's 101 Spells for Every Occasion*. Bursting with useful stuff, this is. Now, if I'm not mistaken…" He leafed through the pages, and Daniel felt hope ballooning in his chest. "Yes, yes here it is!"

He began to read:

Wicker's Finding Spell for the Absent of Mind

Invented by the gifted but forgetful magician Crikey Wicker in 1767, this spell is perfect for anyone cursed with the unfortunate habit of misplacing everyday objects. The spell was lost in the late 1700s when Wicker, who was quite certain that other magicians were intent on stealing his magic, secreted the spell away and proceeded to forget the hiding place. His wife discovered it some years later rolled up in a ball and stuffed in one of Wicker's old socks.

Daniel looked at Ellie.

Ellie looked at Daniel.

"That sounds great," said Ellie politely. "There's just one teeny, tiny thing: that spell sounds like it was made to find lost keys and shoes and things like that. But it's not exactly an everyday object we're looking for."

Mort closed the book and tossed it into the air. It flew back to its place. "Oh, it isn't?"

"No. It's something quite big," said Daniel. "Very big, actually."

"Humongous," added Ellie.

"And it's not just fallen behind some furniture," said Daniel. "In fact, it could be on the other side of the world."

Mort rubbed his chin. "Oh dear. Right. Well, in that case, I'm afraid you're snookered."

"Snookered?"

"Yes. You see, it's a well-known fact that the further away something is, the more powerful the spell must be to affect it. Common sense really, isn't it? A spell to find something that far away would have to be immense! Far, far bigger than anything I've ever even dreamed of trying."

Daniel felt the hope in his chest deflate. "So we can't do anything?"

He was so depressed, so utterly devastated by the thought of never seeing the Nowhere Emporium again, that he sat down on the carpet of the bookstore and buried his face in his arms.

"Come, now, Daniel," said Mort. "It can't be all that bad, can it?"

Daniel looked up at the kindly shopkeeper, and he was embarrassed to feel tears running down his cheeks. He looked away quickly, rubbed his face.

"I wish I could help…" Mort paused. "But I wonder…" He screwed his face up in thought, as though he was deciding whether to tell them something or not.

"Please. We'll try *anything*," Ellie begged.

Mort's eyes flicked from Daniel to Ellie. "Alright. It seems like a desperate situation." He motioned for them to come closer. "There's a witch lives out on one of the islands on the lake." His voice was low, almost a whisper. "Her name's Peg. Some folks say she's two hundred years old. Now, I don't know if that's true, but I know she's powerful. If there's anyone in these parts who can help you, I'd bet on old Peg."

Daniel's heart was a drum in his chest. "Peg? Island? Lake? Thank you! Thank you so much!"

And just like that they were away, pulling open the shop door and racing out into the darkening evening.

"Just be careful!" called the shopkeeper. "Peg doesn't like visitors! And watch out for the trees!"

But it was too late. They were already gone.

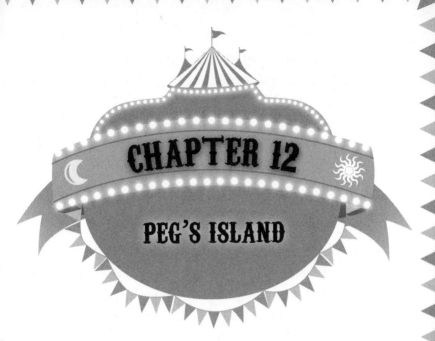

CHAPTER 12

PEG'S ISLAND

Keswick, Present Day

The sky above Keswick was now dark and clear and alive with shimmering stars. Autumn was tightening its grip and Daniel and Ellie's every breath was a curl of silver fog.

Outside the magic district, the town was still busy. The market sellers were packing away their stalls and goods, and warm, inviting light spilled from pubs and restaurants and hotels.

They hurried through the old town, along winding streets, past a park, and at last came to the lake shore.

Without the light from the town, the sky was clearer than ever, and the lake spread out before them, so calm it looked like a sheet of black glass. It was possible, though only just, to squint into the calm, quiet dark and see patches of black rising from the water. Islands.

"Why didn't we ask which island Peg lives on?" said Ellie, a little breathless from running.

"Because," said Daniel, "we're idiots."

"And even if we find out, how do we actually get out there? Look, the ferry is done for the night. Everything's closed up. Everyone's gone home."

Daniel scanned around, walked down the slope of loose stones to the edge of the gently lapping water. There was a wooden jetty where the ferry boats were moored, and behind the ferries…

"There. Look." He pointed. "Rowing boats!"

Ellie stared at him. "Rowing boats that don't belong to us, you mean?"

"It's an emergency. We'll only be borrowing one. We'll put it right back when we're done."

Somewhere across the vast dark expanse of the lake, a series of fireworks exploded in the sky, falling in shimmering sparks. The sight of them made Daniel think of opening night at the Nowhere Emporium, and the ache in his chest intensified.

"You stay here if you like." He marched off towards the rowing boats. "I'm going to find Peg. And I'm going to… get… the Emporium… BACK… what is *wrong* with this rope?"

He was trying to untie a knot in the rope that was mooring one of the small boats to the jetty, but managing to do nothing but tighten it. Suddenly Ellie was at his side, taking the rope in her hands, untying the knot with ease. She gave him a smile.

Daniel glared at the rope and climbed into the boat. The feel of the gentle rocking took him back to the night he'd faced Vindictus Sharpe: the trap Sharpe had set for him in the Emporium, trying to drown him on a fishing boat in a storm. But Daniel's dad had come – from where Daniel didn't know, as his parents had both died when he was a baby – and helped him escape…

"Hello? Still with me?"

Ellie climbed aboard, brought Daniel back to the present.

"Yeah… fine. Can you hand me that oar, please?"

The oars were heavy, and it took a bit of time for Daniel to get the boat moving, but after a while they were cutting through the smooth black water with a bit of speed. It seemed the further they travelled from the land, the deeper the quiet became, and soon the only sound was the rhythmic whoosh of the oars in the water.

Little islands rose up, dark shapes in the night.

The first island they reached was too small to be inhabited by anything other than birds, so they rowed on by. The second was larger, so Daniel took the boat around the outer edge.

"I wonder if this is it?"

"Dunno." Ellie peered into the dense, black woodland. "Doesn't seem like anything could live in there. It's all thorns and overgrown… wait. Look!"

She pointed over Daniel's shoulder, to the sky, and Daniel turned and saw at once what had caught Ellie's attention. Further out in the lake, coils of smoke were drifting up from among the trees on one of the other islands.

"Bingo."

Ten minutes later the boat ran aground on a stony little beach, and Daniel and Ellie hopped out and crept among the trees. The woodland was thick and tangled, the floor a carpet of fallen autumn leaves. There seemed to be no path or trail.

"What's that?" whispered Daniel.

Moonlight was breaking through the trees here and there, and a nearby flash of white had caught Daniel's eye. Someone had nailed a sign to a twisted old trunk. The message had been painted on with a series of violent brush strokes, and there were dribbles of paint all over it.

PRIVAT PROPURTY
TRESSPASSERS WILL BE
CHUKED DOWN THE WELL
THIS MEANS YOU!!!!!!

"Well, she sounds lovely," murmured Ellie behind him.

In the dark, something snapped.

Daniel shivered. Fear had suddenly crept up on him, ambushed him. He felt its cold, scratching fingers on his spine.

Ellie gasped. "Daniel! The trees! Look at the—"

He spun around, and an involuntary sound escaped him: a small, frightened squeal.

The trees were moving, branches twining, reaching, wrapping around Ellie. Daniel had no clue what to do. Panic clogged his throat. He had no plan formed in his head when he went to lunge forward, but in any case it didn't matter, because the trees were wrapping around him too. The branches scratched his skin as he struggled, and as they grasped him tight he was sure they were going to squeeze the air from him, crush him. Ellie was struggling too, and he heard her cries and pants.

"Ellie!"

"Daniel!"

Twigs clutched his face, held his head still, clamped his mouth shut.

And then, as quickly as the trees had begun to move, they stopped. They didn't let go, but simply held Daniel and Ellie, trapping them in the darkness.

Everything in the woodland was still.

In the sudden silence, Daniel heard the gentle

lapping of the lake, heard his own heart and the ragged sound of his lungs sucking in air. For a moment he considered that they might be stuck like this forever, that one day someone else might visit the island and be horrified to find two skeletons entangled in the branches. But then he heard the snap and crack of someone pushing through the trees towards him, muttering.

"… getting an old woman out of bed at this hour… Well, I don't know, do I? That's what I'm about to find out…"

It sounded like the voice was talking to someone else, and Daniel and Ellie could only hear one side of the conversation. But when a woman stepped out from the tangled trees she was alone. As she came closer, the shattered moonlight fell upon half of her face in sharp fragments. The woman was tall with rich ochre skin, and her aged features were so fine that Daniel wondered whether she might once have been a movie star. She looked at him, and then at Ellie.

"Ain't nothin' but a couple kids," she said, as if answering someone close by. "Hold on… I'll ask 'em."

She clicked her fingers and the branches that were holding Daniel's face let go. He gasped, tried to shake the feeling back into his jaw.

The woman came closer. She smelled of trees and earth. "So? What's this? Your little pals dare you to row across here? That what happened?"

Daniel shook his head.

"Or are you tryin' to impress your girlfriend here? That it? You heard the stories and you're tryin' to show her you ain't scared?" She pointed to Ellie and clicked her fingers, and the branches loosened their grip on her face.

"You let us go this minute!" Ellie yelled. "We haven't done anything wrong!"

"Ha!" The woman spat on the ground. "Nothin' wrong…" She stopped, and listened, nodding here and there as if someone was speaking to her. "Oh, don't be ridiculous. They're only kids! I ain't chuckin' 'em down the well!"

Daniel and Ellie stared at each other, wide-eyed, trembling.

"Who are you talking to?" Daniel asked, amazed that he'd found his voice.

The woman stared at him, and smiled. She clicked her fingers again and the branches that were holding Daniel and Ellie suddenly released them, and they fell to the ground.

"Get in your little boat, row ashore, and don't ever come back. If I see you again, I'll listen to *them* and throw you down the well."

Daniel got to his feet, dusted himself off. "Please. We need your help, Peg. That's your name, isn't it? Mr Folio sent us – from the bookshop in the magic district."

She raised an eyebrow. "Mort Folio? Ha! He fancies himself as a bit of a know-it-all that one. But I remember when he was runnin' around in a waterlogged nappy! I don't know what he told you, but I'm not in the business of helping people. I got enough on my plate out here. Too much to worry about."

"You ever heard of the Nowhere Emporium?" Ellie asked.

Peg stared and blinked, and looked up and to the left, as if there was someone sitting in one of the trees conversing with her. "I can't help you."

"It's been stolen," Daniel went on.

"Impossible. I've met the man who runs the place and there ain't a soul ever lived could take his shop from him."

Ellie walked slowly forwards. "You know Papa?"

"Papa? What are you goin' on about?"

"Mr Silver was Ellie's dad," explained Daniel.

Peg's eyes flicked from Daniel to Ellie, and then to the place in the tree where she seemed to think someone else sat.

"*Was*? What d'you mean *was* her dad?"

"He's gone." Ellie looked at the ground. "Passed away."

"I'm in charge now," said Daniel, "and I've gone and stuffed everything up. I've lost the Emporium and I need to get it back. Please help me. Please!"

Peg looked up to the empty trees again. "Well you don't need to tell me that!" she said, then she let out a long sigh and nodded. "You'd best come with me."

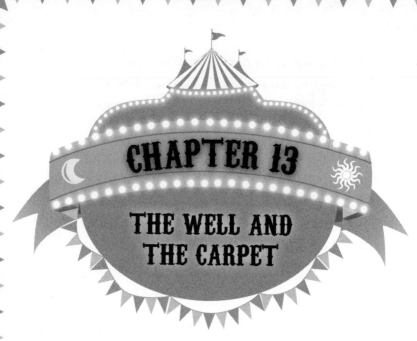

CHAPTER 13

THE WELL AND THE CARPET

Keswick, Present Day

"I know we only have one candle! But I owe Silver a favour, don't I? Oh, state the bleedin' obvious, why don't you? What would you have me do? I've told you I ain't throwin' anyone down the well!"

Peg was arguing, as far as Daniel could tell, with a person who did not exist. They followed her through the tangle of trees and creeping plants, breathing the thick smell of wild garlic and sharing worried glances. After a few minutes they came to a cottage so tightly packed between the trees that it was difficult to tell exactly where the woods ended and the house began.

As they approached the ivy-covered front door,

Daniel caught a glimpse of something in the moonlight off to the side of the cottage. Buried among tangled branches and overgrown wild plants was what looked like a circular stone well.

The night air was freezing cold, but in that moment the temperature seemed to drop even further. From the well came a faraway echoing sound, like a distant rumble of thunder, and on the edges of the rumble, what might have been a scream.

Before he knew what was happening, Peg was pushing past him, stomping towards the well. She leaned on the edge, looked over and called down into the darkness.

"Shut it!"

Then she returned, as if nothing out of the ordinary had happened, and opened the door to her cottage.

There was a single room inside, small and square and quite bare, lit by scattered candles. In one corner was an iron-framed bed, in the other an old-fashioned cooking range. There was a single rocking chair, a simple wooden table and chairs, and a dusty old rug on the floor. No other furniture. No pictures on the walls. No curtains. The only other object of any note was a guitar leaning against one of the bare walls.

"You can't stay here long," said Peg. "This place isn't safe. You shouldn't be here at all. It'll upset the balance."

Ellie was watching her carefully. "How did you know Papa?"

"He came to Keswick a long time ago, when I was a young woman. I went to his shop, and we hit it off." She looked over towards a darkened corner, pointed a finger at nothing. "You keep your comments to yourself! We was friends is all. Nothin' else!" She turned back towards Ellie. "We bonded because we was both different from everyone else. We was outsiders – even in the magic world."

"You said you owe him? Why?"

Peg seemed suddenly to be staring at something far in the distance. "There are more worlds than ours, you know. Infinite worlds, some say, all folded up together and on top of each other. And there's places, see, where the borders are thin. Places like this town, this lake, where things can come through. And when that happens, you need someone to put 'em back where they belong."

"'And that's you?" said Daniel. "That's your job? To put the... things back?"

"Sometimes," said Peg, "they don't want to go back. Sometimes they run. And that cannot be allowed. So I catch 'em, and I put 'em somewhere safe."

Daniel stared out of the window, into the dark. "That's not an ordinary well out there, is it?"

Peg touched the side of her nose, winked. "Clever boy."

"But what does any of that have to do with Papa?" asked Ellie.

Peg looked towards the corner of the room again. "Ain't she just!" she said to nobody.

"What was that?" said Ellie. "What are you saying?"

Peg waved a hand. "Oh, you pay them no attention, love. They're always on the wind up. Always tryin' to stir the pot. Lucien Silver saved my life. That's why I owe him, why I'm helping you."

Ellie became very quiet.

"When was the last time you saw him?" Daniel asked.

"Let me think now… not for many years. Changed over time, he did. You could see somethin' was eating away at him, see that he was frightened. The gaps between his visits grew longer. And then, one day, he just didn't come back."

Daniel shared a knowing look with Ellie; of course they knew the reason Mr Silver had been frightened – Vindictus Sharpe had been chasing him through time and space, determined to kill him, to take his *Book of Wonders*.

When Peg next looked at Daniel, there was great sorrow in her face. "He's really gone?"

"He is."

"I can't believe it. It thought he would go on forever."

"If you've seen the Nowhere Emporium," Daniel said, "you know what it can do. You know how much

95

power is in there. We can't have it on the loose or under someone else's control. We have to find it."

Peg nodded. Then she turned to an empty patch of room and frowned as if someone was saying something quite disagreeable. "Well, of course I won't be goin' with 'em! You think I'd leave the island? Leave the well unguarded? Who knows what would happen!"

"Sorry," said Daniel, who was beginning to feel like he was the crazy one. "Go where?"

"Edinburgh," said Peg. "That's where you have to go. There's a magician there who can help you. This island and the well and the job I have to do… all my strength's tied up in that. And it's finely balanced. If I were to cast the kind of spell you need, it might throw everything into chaos. We can't have that."

She looked exhausted as she turned away, went to the corner of the room, and to Daniel's great surprise, crouched low and pulled up one of the floorboards revealing a dark hollow. She reached in, brought out something cylindrical wrapped in brown paper, then she slotted the floorboard back in place. "A friend gave me this a long time ago," she said, unwrapping the object.

Daniel stared down at it. "It's a candle."

And so it was – a fat candle the colour of vanilla ice cream.

"It's a candle that's going to help you find your way

home," said Peg. "Now, like I said, I can't burn it here. It's too powerful and the island is unstable. There's only one other person I'd trust to burn it properly, 'cause it takes power to do it right. You need to get to Edinburgh. To this place…" She went to the table, opened a drawer, took out a piece of paper and a pen, scrawled something down, folded up the paper, and gave it to Daniel. "That's where you'll find him. You tell him Peg sent you, that it's important, and he'll do the rest."

"There's just one problem with this plan," said Ellie. "How do we get to Edinburgh? We've no money, no transport…"

Peg held up a finger. "That, my love, is where you're wrong." She snapped her fingers again, like she'd done to control the trees.

Daniel's eyes were drawn to the floor, where something strange was happening. The dusty old rug was moving. First its corners twitched, and then a ripple passed through it, throwing dust into the air, making Daniel and Ellie sneeze. It floated up off the floorboards, and hung in the air for a long moment before tearing off around the room, streaking past Daniel, swooping low over Ellie's dark curls.

"A magic carpet!" Daniel felt himself smiling, despite all of the worries weighing on him. "I saw a shop selling these in Cairo, but they were all rolled up and sitting in rows. I've never seen one actually fly!"

Ellie crept forward, crouched down and poked the carpet with a finger. "Were going to fly to Edinburgh on *this?*"

Daniel shrugged. "You got any better ideas?"

Five minutes later they were back on the island's stony little beach. The night was still and cold, and the clear full moon reflected on the glassy surface of the lake.

Peg held the carpet under her arm, then she unrolled it and let it fall. It straightened out in a flash, sat floating in the air.

Daniel felt like a small child on Christmas morning. He was bursting with excitement as he climbed on.

"That's it," said Peg. "One leg at a time. Just sit any way that's comfortable."

It was a strange sensation, climbing onto the magic carpet. It felt a little like sitting on a boat, only instead of moving with the water, the carpet rose and fell with the currents of the breeze.

Daniel took Ellie's arm and helped her aboard. "How do we drive it?"

"Easy as pie," said Peg. "You just say the name of the place you want to go and the carpet does the rest. When you want to land, just say so."

"You mean all I have to say is 'Edinburgh'—"

The carpet shot up into the air with such speed that everything was a blur. In just a matter of moments they were so high that the lake was a patch of black that Daniel could cover with a single hand, and the lights of Keswick seemed as distant as the stars.

At first, as they tore across the sky, Daniel gripped the carpet so tightly his hands were sore, but soon he realised that as fast as the carpet was moving, he could let go and wouldn't fall off. Some magical force was keeping him on.

"Ellie!" he cried. "Let go!" He spread out his arms.

"You're mental! We aren't in one of your Wonders now! We can actually die out here!"

"I know that! Just… trust me… let go!"

Ellie closed her eyes and released her grip on the magic carpet, and Daniel laughed.

"See? It won't let you fall."

Ellie opened one eye, then the other, and smiled, then laughed. Soon they were kneeling up on the carpet as it swooped through the night, the wind in their faces and their hair, the clouds spread out below like an ocean of cotton wool.

CHAPTER 14

THE MESSAGE IN THE FLAMES

Mayfair, London, 1967

Kenworth, the butler of Number 120 Park Street, which served as the headquarters for the Bureau of Magical Investigation, entered the grand drawing room and gave a stiff bow. The armchairs were grand and deep and leathery, and the room smelled of cigar smoke. In three of the armchairs sat Mr Ivy, Mrs Hennypeck and young Flintwitch, all deep in concentration.

"Hem hem."

"Yes, Kenworth?"

"I thought I'd enquire whether you'd like any refreshments, sir. You've been in here a while."

"Ah. Yes, good idea. The usual for me, please."

"Very good, sir. And Master Flintwitch?"

Flintwitch licked his lips. "I'd love a milkshake. Strawberry. With whipped cream."

Kenworth raised an overgrown eyebrow. "Is that all, sir?"

Flintwitch thought about this. "Do you have any sprinkles?"

"Sprinkles? I shall have to check, sir."

He then turned to Mrs Hennypeck, and there was a moment of awkward silence.

"I won't be requiring anything," she said. "On account of the fact I'm dead."

"Yes, ma'am." Kenworth left the room in a most dignified manner.

"Are you quite alright, Mrs Hennypeck?" asked Mr Ivy.

The old woman's face was set in a mask of deep concern, and she worried away at a jewel on her necklace.

"It's just a bit of an adjustment, you know? Being back after all this time, and seeing magicians I've worked with – good folks – meet their end like this…"

Kenworth reappeared, carrying a tray upon which sat a crystal glass filled with ice and amber liquid for Mr Ivy, and a tall strawberry milkshake with all the trimmings for Flintwitch.

"Who'd be crazy enough to go after former Bureau Investigators?" said Flintwitch, taking a gulp of his shake, which left a tremendous whipped cream moustache on his upper lip. "They may have been retired, but they were still pretty powerful magicians, right?"

Mr Ivy took a sip from his glass, breathed in through his teeth. "Indeed. I've been thinking… the most likely scenario is that someone – or something – the Bureau dealt with in the past has returned with a score to settle. These investigators would all have served in your time, Mrs Hennypeck. Any thoughts on who might hold a grudge?"

"That crossed my mind too," she said. "I've been trying to remember… but…" She shook her head. "Being dead, you see, makes it so much more difficult to remember things. There's something… way in the back of my mind… but I can't quite grasp it."

Mr Ivy nodded. "I'm sure it'll come back to you."

There was a whistling sound from the fireplace, like wind blowing down the chimney, but outside all was perfectly still. Coal dust fell into the fire from above, and then a blur of tiny glowing objects came whooshing out of the chimney, through the flames and into the drawing room. The objects were letters and words, all jumbled up, entangled and entwined, glowing white-hot. They swirled around Mr Ivy, melding together and arranging themselves in sentences as paper began to form around the words, until there was a letter floating in mid-air. The letter drifted down into Mr Ivy's hands, and he took a moment to read it. Then he looked at the others, his expression grim.

"Finish that milkshake, Flintwitch, you'll need your strength. There has been another attack."

CHAPTER 15

SPARK OF ANGER

The Nowhere Emporium, Somewhere in Time and Space

Edna Bloom sat on the dry grass of the Carnival of Wonders, tears rolling down her face. The part of her that was crying wanted to go home, wanted to see her mum, wanted to sit at the boring old dinner table and eat boring old food and have the same boring old conversations as always. But the other part of Edna, the out-of-control part that had stolen the Nowhere Emporium, told her that she could never go back. *Not now – how could I? I'm a thief! They'd lock me up. Besides, I haven't found the Fountain yet…*

"Have to find the Fountain. The Fountain…"

She stood up, though her legs ached, and began to walk again.

How many miles have I covered? Ten? Twenty?

The sound of splashing water filled her head, and she swung around, listening, straining to hear where it was coming from…

There!

She dashed forward in such a hurry she tripped and fell, then climbed up and kept running towards a yellow-striped tent, crashing through the entrance.

She did not see a fountain.

She saw a lazy stream bubbling past, with fish leaping, leaving rainbow trails in the air before they splashed back into the water.

That's pretty, thought part of Edna.

No, thought another part. *No, it's not. It's useless! It's foolish and pointless! It's not the Fountain!*

Anger bubbled up inside her, reached boiling point and spilled out into every part of her. She stomped out of the tent, not at all sure why she was so furious, and by the time she was back out in the carnival her fingertips were smoking hot, sparks of magic jumping between her fingers.

"What's happening to me?" she screamed in confusion and anger, and a sparking jet of pure magic leapt from her fingers, hit the tent she'd come from, and set it alight. The flames grew, and the fire spewed black smoke into the twilight carnival sky.

As the tent burned, Edna stared at her shadow and, for a moment, thought she could hear it laughing.

CHAPTER 16

SPARROW'S CLOSE

Edinburgh, Present Day

It had begun as a thrill ride, but by the time the carpet reached Edinburgh, Daniel and Ellie were half-frozen and desperate to feel solid ground beneath their feet.

It was now the middle of the night, and Edinburgh was dusted in frost that twinkled in the light of the clear full moon. From the sky, they could see a vast web of winding, narrow streets stretching off in all directions. Almost everything was still; there were only a few cars on the road, and even fewer people walking about.

The carpet lowered them gently towards the looming shape of Edinburgh Castle, and touched down in a shadowy corner of the deserted High Street. They climbed off, stretching and groaning, and Ellie took a few paces and looked about.

"This is where Papa was born."

"It is, isn't it?" said Daniel. "I hadn't thought about that."

Ellie touched the wall of the nearest building. "He might have walked down this street. Probably stood in this very spot!" She shook her head. "I wish I'd made more of an effort to get to know him – the *real* him."

Daniel said nothing, because what was there to say? He knew how she felt, was only too familiar with the pain and anger and sadness running through her. Those same feelings had grabbed hold of him many times back in the children's home where he had lived before he met Mr Silver, and still not a day went by that he didn't think of his parents, wonder about them, wish he'd had the chance to know them better.

The sound of a faraway siren shook them awake.

"Right," said Daniel. "This isn't getting us anywhere." He reached into his pocket, brought out the candle wrapped in brown paper, and unwrapped it to reveal Peg's message:

Sparrows Close Clokmaker
Giv im the candel

"Sparrow's Close," he said, more to himself than to Ellie. There was a flicker of recognition in his mind, but he couldn't turn it into anything more.

In a moment, they were back on the carpet, Daniel to the front, Ellie the rear, and Daniel had stowed the candle away once more. "Sparrow's Close," he told the carpet, which rippled under them, lifted from the ground and carried them up through the cold light of the moon.

They returned to the ground a few streets away between two rows of high, proud stone buildings. Daniel rolled up the magic carpet and slung it over his shoulder, and they began to study the names of the various closes – narrow alleyways leading off the main street.

Advocate's Close...

Anchor Close...

Trunk's Close...

And then, ah! Sparrow's Close!

It looked, upon first glance, no different to the others – a gloomy doorway in the stone leading through to a darkened passageway. But after they'd entered and had begun to walk cautiously through the passage, the darkness became thicker, until it was so black that Daniel couldn't see the end of his own nose. The air changed, became charged and heavy with the scents of burning paraffin, liquorice and sawdust.

And then, up ahead, a warm glow coming from a square window in the passageway wall, a dead end.

Daniel and Ellie approached the window. There was no glass, only a hole in the wall, and beyond it a small room barely the size of a broom cupboard. Sitting at the window was a bored-looking man in a crisp bottle-green uniform, but when he saw them emerge from the dark, the boredom was replaced by surprise.

"Hello, hello. You two know what time it is?"

"We do," said Daniel.

The man leaned back in his chair. "And do you make a habit of sneaking around the city in the dead of night?"

"It's an emergency," said Ellie.

Then man pursed his lips. "Right. Anything to declare?"

"What?"

The man spoke slowly this time. "Do. You. Have. Anything. To. Declare?"

Daniel looked at Ellie, and she stared back at him and shrugged.

"OK… I… um… I like your hat?" replied Daniel.

The man shook his head.

"No! Declare!" He jabbed his finger repeatedly down on the counter. "It means are you bringing anything foreign into the magic district? Temporary regulations, y'see, on account of an incident a few weeks back. Some idiot thought it would be a good idea to bring a tank of storm wasps into the country! Some of 'em escaped, of course, and went buzzin' around the streets shootin' lightning out their backsides! Took days to catch 'em all."

There was a moment of silence, until Daniel realised the man was expecting him to react in some way to his story.

"Oh! That's terrible," he said at last.

"You're telling me!" said the man.

"Well, you don't have to worry about us, does he, Ellie? All we have is this old thing." He indicated the magic carpet rolled up on his shoulder.

"Right." The man rummaged somewhere down below the window and brought out a sheet of paper. Then he reached into the chest pocket of his bottle-green jacket and put on a pair of round spectacles. He squinted at the paper. "Let me see now. Yes, here we are. To the best of your knowledge, has the item in question been cursed or enchanted to cause bodily harm, up to and including death?"

"What? No!" said Ellie. "At least I hope not."

The man made a mark on the paper.

"To your knowledge, did the object originate in the continent of South America? And if so, has it been properly inspected for traces of Fire Beetle eggs or Spear-tailed Dragon Toad saliva?"

Daniel wondered for a moment whether the man

might be joking, but the look on his face was deadly serious, so he said, "Um… Cairo. Peg said the carpet came from Cairo."

The man nodded, marked the paper again, then stamped it with red ink that said **APPROVED**, and passed it through the window.

"Right. That's you. You can go through."

"Through where?" said Daniel. "It's a dead end—"

It *had* been a dead end.

But it wasn't any more.

Straight ahead, where there had been a wall, was now an opening, a narrow passage in the stone revealing the flickering oil lamps of a magical street.

"On you go, then!" said the man in the window.

Daniel gave him a nod, and another to Ellie, and they walked side by side down the passage beyond.

CHAPTER 17

HEARTS OF STONE

The Nowhere Emporium, Somewhere in Time and Space

Caleb, the barrel-chested fire-breather, sat at a table in the tavern tent of the Emporium staff's private campsite. He finished his mug of ale, wiped the foam from his moustache, and stared at the playing cards in his big hands.

There were two others at the table: Anja, the tall snake charmer, who wore a live silver snake around her neck like a necklace, and the metal Ringmaster from the Iron Circus.

Caleb stared at the cards, then he huffed and threw them into the air. Before they could flutter back down, he breathed out a huge tongue of fire, incinerating the cards; they rained down in small clouds of ash.

"Not again, Caleb!" said Anja.

The Ringmaster wagged a metal finger. "You really must learn to be a better loser. You can't go destroying half the deck every time you're dealt a bum hand!"

Caleb looked up, spotted something out of the window. "Smoke. I see smoke."

"Well, of course you see smoke!" said Anja. "You've just set the cards on fire."

"No! Not in here. Out there. Look." He pointed out of the window, where a column of black smoke was rising into the sky somewhere far off in the Carnival of Wonders.

"That can't be good. We should do—" The Ringmaster stopped talking, because Caleb and Anja were already halfway to the door. The Ringmaster jumped up, fixed on his iron hat and chased after them.

Through passageways between tents they charged, following the great column of black smoke in the sky, passing Wonders all the while: Leap of Faith, Fire Garden, Emerald Lagoon, Library of Souls. Past the great bog top of the Iron Circus, further and further out into the sprawling, never-ending city of tents, until, at last, they came upon a huge wall of flame. Several tents were burning and the flames were spreading over the dry summer grass too, licking higher and higher.

Caleb and Anja shielded their faces from the intense heat.

The Ringmaster, being made of iron, had no such trouble. He walked towards the flames, pointing. "Someone's in there! In the fire!"

"Be careful!" shouted Anja, but he was already in the flames, moving towards the figure… a girl wearing glasses, seemingly unaffected by the fire.

The Ringmaster grabbed her and dragged her out. "Are you alright? What happened?"

The girl didn't answer. She stared at the fire, seemed to be looking straight through it, somewhere far away.

Caleb and Anja came rushing over.

"We must put the fire out!" shouted Caleb.

"I'm looking for the Fountain," said the girl calmly. "Do you know where it is?"

"The Fountain?" Caleb and Anja shared a puzzled look. How could she know about the Fountain?

"I really need to get to the Fountain. Please don't get in my way."

"Your way?" Caleb's voice boomed. "If it wasn't for the Ringmaster you'd have been barbecued!"

"Where's Mr Daniel?" the Ringmaster asked, the cogs and gears of his metal face spinning and clicking.

"He should be here…" said Anja. "Young lady, does Daniel know you're here?"

The girl stared back in a blank, slightly dreamy sort of way. She pointed. "Is the Fountain that way?"

"Forget the Fountain." Caleb looked more and more uneasy. "We need to get you to the shopfront, to Daniel and Ellie. They'll fix this. They'll get you home."

"That's right," said Anja, and she gave the girl a warm smile. "You want to get home, don't you, dear?"

Of course I do, thought part of Edna. *Of course I want to get home. I don't know what's happening to me. I don't know why I'm doing these things.*

But that other part of her, the part that seemed only to have popped into existence after she'd entered the Nowhere Emporium, spoke louder and more persuasively. *The Fountain. I need the Fountain.* Heat crackled at her fingertips again.

Caleb had had enough. He reached out – perhaps to take the girl by the hand, perhaps to lift her up and carry her all the way to the exit. But before either of those things could happen, his hand stopped moving. He stared disbelievingly as first his fingertips, then his knuckles, then his wrist turned to stone. The stone crept up his arm, reached his shoulder, spread over his body, his legs, his feet. The creeping stone reached Caleb's neck, began to crawl up his face. His mouth was frozen in terror, his eyes wide. With one final breath he became a statue, cold and still.

"Caleb!" Anja called out, but the snake around her neck was already stone, and before she had a chance to move, the stone took her too.

Silence.

Edna stood almost as still as the statues she'd created. There was a look of serene calm on her smoke-smudged face, but inside her head was a very different story. The two opposing parts of her were fighting.

I must turn them back. This isn't me! I don't do things like this! Not me? Then who is it? I can't turn them back – they'll turn me in. After I've found the Fountain. It'll all be better then. I can make it all go away. I can get my life back...

Edna began to walk, but halted in front of the clockwork ringmaster. She looked him up and down. He had not turned to stone like the others; he was still all metal gears and cogs, but the glow that had flickered behind the glass lenses of his eyes was gone. She reached out, knocked on his face, *clank clank clank*, and then kicked him, *CLANG*, on the leg. He didn't move. There wasn't a flicker of light in his eyes or a click in his gears. He seemed quite broken.

So Edna moved on, away from the fire and the statues, in search of the Fountain once again.

Only when the girl was gone did the Ringmaster's eyes flicker to life. The clockwork gears of his body sparked into motion, spinning and clicking.

He did not know why, or how, but he had not turned to stone like the others. His clockwork mind had been quick enough to realise that he must pretend to be bewitched, and it had worked.

"I'll bring you back," he said quietly to the statues of his friends, Caleb and Anja. "I'll find a way."

He tipped his iron hat to them and walked after the girl, making sure to keep to the shadows.

CHAPTER 18

THE CLOCKMAKER

Magic District, Edinburgh, Present Day

When the passageway opened up, Daniel and Ellie found themselves standing in an old lane built on a steep hill. The entrance, where they stood now, was at the crest of the hill, and the magic district rolled out before them. There was a stretch of cobbled path, and then a series of steps down to the next stretch, and then more steps, and on it went. Lining either side were tall crooked tenement buildings. The ground floor of the buildings mostly comprised of shops and pubs. The dwellings above sometimes reached eight storeys up towards the sky, and there were washing lines scattered with all manner of interesting garments strung high across the alleyway.

The entire place was quiet and still, and the cold full moon shone down and mingled with the honey-coloured warmth of paraffin lamps.

"C'mon then." Ellie walked ahead, scanning the shop signs. "What did you say Peg wrote on that paper? Clockmaker?"

On they went, their feet soft on the cobbles.

What a sight this place must be in daytime, thought Daniel. He imagined the lane alive with people, with smells of street food and spells and ingredients. He found himself wishing the sun would rise just so he could see it in full flow.

They moved quickly along each stretch of lane, down the steps and then on to the next, past a blacksmith and an apothecary, a museum of magical artefacts and a coffee house, all closed and silent.

Then…

"There! Found it!" Daniel's voice was an excited whisper.

The shop was small, with a single window on one side of the door, and a green and gold sign above.

"What now?" said Ellie.

Daniel didn't answer at first, because he had been thinking the same thing. It was after three in the morning, but he was tired and freezing and wanted his Emporium back. He knocked on the shop door, *bang bang bang*!

No one answered.

He knocked again.

BANG BANG BANG!

"Will you keep it down out there! I'm trying to sleep!"

The voice had come from across the lane, high in one of the tenement buildings.

"How about *you* keep it down, Franco!" came a second voice from a window above. "I'm up early for work and the last thing I need is your foghorn voice wakin' me up!"

"The pair of you button it or I'll turn your tongues into slugs!" a third voice interjected.

"Slugs, he says! Ha! You couldnae turn a corner!"

"Why don't you come say that to my face, eh?"

"Well, I might!"

Daniel was wondering whether the back and forth would ever end when a glimmer of movement caught his eye. He looked at the windows of the first floor flat above the clockmaker's shop and saw the curtains twitch. A man's face appeared, with very weathered sepia-brown skin, a square jaw and a thick layer of stubble on his chin. He was wearing a nightcap, which seemed to be too big, because it kept sliding down over his eyes. He looked up and around at the tenements across the lane, and then down at Daniel and Ellie, and when he saw them his thick eyebrows raised up. With a jerk of the curtains he was gone.

A moment later, through the window of the shop, Daniel noticed the warm glow of candlelight, heard muffled footsteps. Then there was the scratch and click of a key and locks and bolts, and the door to the shop creaked open just enough to show the man's face. He stared out at them, then past them, down the lane.

"Who's sent you?" he said. "Was it Jimmy the Hangman? It was, wasn't it? You tell him I'll have his money by the end of the week…"

"Jimmy the Hangman didn't send us," said Daniel.

"No? Then who?"

"Peg. Peg sent us."

The man's eyes widened. "Peg?"

"You do know her, don't you?" said Daniel.

"Lives on an island?" said Ellie. "Guards a mystical well? Talks to people who aren't there?"

"Course I know who she is," said the man. "She's my sister." He shook his head. "But she didn't send you. She wouldn't send anyone to me. This is a trick! Somebody's trying to get in my head…"

Daniel reached into his pocket and brought out

the candle. "She gave us this. Said we were to show it to you and you'd know what to do."

The man stared down at the candle and seemed to sway; for a second Daniel thought he was going to collapse and made ready to catch him through the gap in the door. But he steadied himself, and when he looked into Daniel's eyes again there was something in his expression that had not been there before.

Fear.

"You best come in."

CHAPTER 19

TRAVELLING BY FLAME

Magic District, Edinburgh, Present Day

The clockmaker's door opened wide enough that Daniel and Ellie could slip through into the shop, and suddenly the soft sound of tick-tocking surrounded them.

"Here. Sit."

The man brought a couple of wooden chairs over and lit a few lamps. The light was warm and golden, and all about the workshop it caught on the watches and clocks, on their smooth glass faces and their gold casings, on the cogs and springs laid out precisely on workbenches, so that the entire place glistened and sparkled.

"You came all the way from Keswick on *that?*" The man nodded to the rolled-up carpet at Daniel's feet. "You must be frozen! I'll make some tea." He disappeared and they heard him clanging around upstairs in the flat above the shop. When he returned, he was carrying three steaming mugs. The tea was sweet and hot, and Daniel was thankful for it.

"You look alike," said Daniel, "you and Peg."

The man sipped his tea. He looked at Daniel over his cup. "Name's Arthur. How is she?"

"Lonely, I think," said Ellie. "Though I get the feeling she'd never admit it."

"Sounds about right," said Arthur. To Daniel's great surprise, he sniffed and wiped his eyes. "I tried to visit, you know. Many times. But she wouldn't have it. Wouldn't see me." He set his mug down and leaned forward in his chair, his elbows on his knees, his hands together. "We were so close when we were young. Twins, see. Then she took that job. They offered it to both of us, you know. But I didn't want any part of it. I wanted to get out in the world and live, and I told Peg she should do the same. But she wouldn't listen. She wanted to help, y'see. Wanted to prove how strong she was. So off she went, and she's been there ever since, and I can't think about her without picturing her all alone in that place, between worlds, surrounded by dark things."

The ticking of the clocks filled the quiet again, like whispering voices.

"She hasn't forgotten you," said Daniel. "She sent us here, told us you were the only one strong enough to help us."

Arthur dabbed at his eyes again. "What exactly is it you need help with?"

Daniel told him about the Nowhere Emporium, and about Peg, and about the candle.

Arthur took the candle, unwrapped it, and examined it.

"I've only ever seen one of these. Powerful things. The night Peg went to her island for the first time, she had to burn one of these. It changed her, made her more than a magician, more than a human…"

Daniel stared at the candle. "What are *we* going to do with it?"

"Burn it, of course."

"Yeah, but what'll happen then?"

Arthur sat the candle on one of his workbenches, scattering cogs and dials, and fetched some matches. He struck one, the flame lighting his face from beneath.

"Something excellent."

He held the match to the wick, and the candle began to burn.

The flame was black.

Daniel couldn't take his eyes off it as it spat and

fizzed and showered the workbench in sparks. The place filled with thick smoke that smelled of hot metal, and Daniel and Ellie covered their mouths.

A blazing circle of light erupted from the floor in the centre of the smoke, and the room crackled and filled with powerful energy, made Daniel's hair stand on end. The floor trembled.

Daniel looked at Ellie. Ellie looked at Daniel. They both looked at Arthur.

"We have to go in *there?*" Daniel pointed down at the circle.

Arthur nodded amiably.

"If you want to find the Emporium, this is the only way. Oh! Wait!"

He turned, went to one of his workbenches, and rummaged in a cupboard. Then he came forward and handed Daniel and Ellie each a length of barky twig.

"Hazel," he said. "Picked at midnight. Comes in handy against things from… other places."

Daniel nodded, and stowed the twig away in his coat. Then he turned his attention back to the blazing circle on the floor.

"Best hurry," said Arthur, indicating the candle. "It's more'n halfway burnt already."

As Daniel stared into the light, he began to see strange shimmers in the air, whispers of colour and glimpses of another place, of a narrow street lined with buildings.

"I think it's a gateway," he said. "I can see through to somewhere else!"

Ellie stood next to him. "I see it too!"

"There's not much candle left," said Arthur. "Go now."

Daniel and Ellie nodded to each other, and Ellie took Daniel's hand. Immediately he felt braver, felt that he could walk anywhere, do anything.

Together, they stepped into the circle.

"Good luck!" shouted Arthur.

A great wind began to blow, so powerful Daniel thought Arthur's workshop would surely be torn apart, but he peered through the light and was amazed to see that outside the circle the world was calm and still. There stood Arthur, sipping his cup of tea, watching as if he had seen this a hundred times before.

There was a harsh ripping sound, and suddenly the ring of light at their feet exploded upwards, encasing them in a tunnel of light. The heat from it was intense, like standing near an open oven.

Daniel tightened his grip, felt Ellie's hand tighten around his. The gale became so wild, the light so bright, that Daniel was sure the world was ripping apart at the seams.

Then it was gone.

It took a few moments for the ringing to leave his ears, for his eyes to become accustomed to the dim light, and when his senses had fully returned Daniel looked at Ellie, and at the place where they now stood.

They were not in Arthur's clockmaking workshop in Edinburgh any more, but standing in a narrow street lit by electric streetlamps. A haze of mist and fine rain hung in the air. There was nobody about. The street was lined on either side with shops and cafes, but their shutters were drawn, and there was no sign of anyone awake in the flats above the shops.

The sound of an engine, and a black cab came around the corner and almost hit them, skidding to a stop on the puddle-soaked road. The driver sounded the horn, rolled down his window and yelled a curse at them, then drove off.

"The same to you!" Ellie called after him.

"Shut up. We don't want to draw attention to…"

He stopped mid-sentence, because something a little further up the street had caught his eye. He took a few steps, hardly daring to believe, his insides fluttering and turning loops.

There, sandwiched between a travel agent and a dry-cleaner, black bricks sparkling and twinkling in the orange glow of the streetlights, was the Nowhere Emporium.

He took off, sprinting up the street, hardly able to contain his joy. He could not wait to get back inside, to feel the familiar, comforting heat of the fire, to be among his friends and his Wonders again.

He stopped at the door, pressed his hand against the wood, and turned to Ellie, who'd caught up with him. "You think it's safe to go in?"

Ellie shrugged. "You're the expert."

That's the trouble, thought Daniel. *I'm not an expert at all. Mr Silver went away before I really had the chance to learn anything properly. I'm making everything up as I go, and sooner or later I'm going to be found out.*

He tried to give the impression he was calm and confident. He nodded at the Emporium door. "Let's go."

The touch of the handle was warming, and when the door opened, the familiar scents of the Emporium shop spilled out and wrapped around Daniel like a hug.

"Edna? Edna, are you here?" he called.

There was no reply.

Daniel stood very still and concentrated.

"What're you doing?"

He held up a finger to quiet Ellie.

"Feeling," he said.

It was a difficult thing to describe, but when he'd taken control of the shop, it had seemed to creep into his thoughts and feelings, and whenever he was inside the Nowhere Emporium, it felt as much a part of him as his nose or his ear. He was still getting the hang of it, but if he concentrated, Daniel could tell how many people were in the shop and what Wonders they were visiting.

"Something isn't right." He concentrated harder, closing his eyes tight.

"Is it Edna?" Ellie asked.

Daniel probed with his mind, felt his way through the carnival, and suddenly saw an enormous wall of leaping flames and burning canvas and blackened grass. A feeling crashed over him, like an icy hand had reached into him and grabbed his heart. He swayed, dropped to his knees.

"Daniel!" Ellie helped him up, guided him to her father's old desk in the corner of the shop and steered him into the chair. "What happened? You're shaking!"

"Fire," he said, his senses returning. "The carnival is on fire!"

CHAPTER 20

DEEP TROUBLE

The Nowhere Emporium, London, Present Day

Daniel and Ellie tore around the corner, their footsteps thumping on the grass, and skidded to a stop, staring up, hardly able to process what they were seeing.

The usual twilight stillness of the Carnival of Wonders had been ripped apart by a hungry inferno; flames had engulfed a huge number of tents, and thick black smoke was billowing out, filling the air.

Daniel acted quickly, bringing out the *Book of Wonders*, opening it to a blank page and scribbling hurriedly on the paper. As he wrote, a change came across the part of the sky directly above;

black clouds gathered, and a torrent of rain came crashing down. In minutes the great fire was out, the rain stopped and the sky cleared.

Daniel and Ellie stood side by side, staring at the burnt carcases of the tents. And then Daniel caught sight of something else through the smoke – the unmistakeable figures of Caleb and Anja. He ran to them, but as the smoke cleared he slowed, until he was standing, open-mouthed in front of them. He reached out and touched Caleb's hand, cold and hard and lifeless.

"Stone. They've turned to stone!"

"How?" Ellie's voice wavered as she stroked Anja's arm. "What's going on, Daniel?"

Daniel didn't answer. He couldn't. Instead, he opened the *Book of Wonders* again, turned to a blank page and began to write:

Caleb and Anja will come back to life at once.

Normally, whenever Daniel wrote something down in the *Book of Wonders*, it would come true in seconds; the book was, as far as he knew, the ultimate power within the boundaries of the Emporium. Nothing he'd ever seen had disputed that fact.

Until now.

Daniel watched, at first with great curiosity then shock and fear, as the words he'd written began to fizz and spark. The letters jumped, literally leapt off the page and fell on the floor, where they bubbled and turned to nothing but inky stains in the blackened grass. Daniel gawped at the book, at the place on the blank page where his words had been, and his insides seemed to tie up in knots.

"That's impossible," he murmured in shock. "That can't happen!"

"Can you tell me where the Fountain is please?"

Daniel and Ellie swivelled round.

"Edna?"

"Edna!"

She stood a few metres away, swaying slightly.

"I'm fine. I just… I need to find the Fountain."

Daniel narrowed his eyes, took a step towards her. There was something very wrong; this wasn't the same wide-eyed teenage girl he'd met only yesterday. That girl had been full of wonder and happiness. This girl, the one who stood before him now, was a shell. Her eyes seemed empty, far away.

Daniel reached out a hand.

"Mr Daniel! Stay back! She's dangerous!" The Ringmaster from the Iron Circus was suddenly between Daniel and Edna, the cogs and gears of his face arranged in a rough impression of anger. "She turned the others to stone. All of them. She set the place on fire!"

Daniel's gaze went to Edna. "Is that true?"

Her eyes, magnified by her thick glasses, brimmed with tears. "I didn't mean to… I just… I need to get to the Fountain."

Daniel took another step forward. "Why? Why do you need to get to the Fountain, Edna?"

She screwed up her face in concentration, closed her eyes, shook her head. "I… I… don't know."

Daniel inched closer. "It's OK. I know… I know you didn't mean to take the Emporium. That's right, isn't it?"

She nodded, and the tears were streaming now.

"Take my hand. We'll get you home. This will all be over."

A pause.

Edna began to reach out. But then she stopped. Her hand dropped back down to her side. "I want to go home," she said, "but I can't… not until I've found the Fountain."

Sparks shot from her fingertips, leapt across the warm air at Daniel. Instinctively he held up the *Book of Wonders* to shield his face, and the sparks hit the book. A sound like thunder shook the whole Emporium. A jolt of heat and pain smashed Daniel in the chest, and he went flying through the air and landed with a painful thump a few metres away.

The Ringmaster and Ellie ran over and helped him up. His blood felt too hot, and his ears were ringing.

"I'm fine." He looked past Ellie, stared around the place. "Where is she? Where did Edna go?"

The only sign that she had ever been there was a pair of scorched footprints in the grass.

Edna Bloom stepped through the red velvet curtain into the shopfront of the Nowhere Emporium. She hurried towards the front door, reached for the handle and paused. She looked back at the curtain.

"What am I doing?" she said. "I have to go back, let them take me home, tell them I think I'm sick. I can't let anyone else get hurt…"

"You're not sick, Edna."

She took a sharp breath, spun around. "Who's that? Is someone here?"

"Look down. Look at the floor."

"Down? What am I supposed to—"

She staggered back, falling into a table, scattering coins and jewels and treasures. On the floor, cast by lamplight, was her shadow. Only now it was changing shape, growing, becoming something else.

Edna stared in horrified disbelief. Her shadow was now the shadow of a man, tall and thin, wearing a top hat. The shadow's head turned towards her.

"I know you must be frightened, Edna," he said, his voice raspy, like he'd smoked too much. "I'm frightened too."

Somehow, Edna didn't believe him. "I want to go home."

"I want that too," said the shadow man. "That's all I want. And we can both have that. But we'll need to work together."

Edna shook her head. "Please leave me alone."

"I wish I could, but I'm trapped…"

"Daniel could help you. He's a great magician."

"We can't trust him, Edna. You think he'll forgive you so easily for stealing his shop?"

"But he said—"

"He was lying, Edna. People lie. It's what they're best at. Do you think they'll believe you when you go back and tell them there's a man living in your shadow? Of course not! They'll blame you, send you to prison. Or worse…" A pause. "What would that do to your poor mum, Edna? She's already lost your grandpa and your dad. What would happen to her if she lost you too?"

Edna took off her soot-smeared glasses, dabbed at her eyes. "I'm so tired."

"I know. But we're almost there. I just need a little more strength to be free. And then I'll make sure everything is sorted. You can go home."

"Is that… is that what the Fountain is? Power?"

"Yes. But we can't have that. Not yet. Daniel's back, and he's strong. We need something else first. Something that'll give us just enough. Then we can come back and set everything right. I want to go home just as much as you do, Edna. Do we have a deal?"

Edna put her glasses back on and brushed the hair from her face. What choice did she have?

She nodded.

"Good," said the man in her shadow.

"Where do we need to go?"

"I'll tell you on the way."

Edna reached out and opened the door, and she and her shadow stepped into the London night.

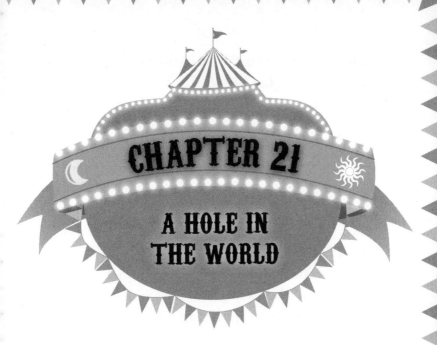

CHAPTER 21

A HOLE IN THE WORLD

London, 1967

It was after one in the morning, and London was mostly still. Occasionally the Rolls Royce Phantom would pass a group of swaying drunks spilling out of a club in their brightly coloured clothes, or meet the lights of a taxi, but for the most part the city slept, the streets and buildings taking time to breathe before the morning brought chaos and traffic and a million hurried pairs of feet.

"Just look at those short skirts," said Mrs Hennypeck in a disapproving tone as the Phantom sped past the entrance to a trendy club. "You can see their knees! And the men! Some of them have longer hair than the women!"

"It's fashion," Flintwitch shrugged. He was ten years old, but he dressed smartly in the mod style, wearing a sharply cut suit and a long, high-collared coat. He was growing his tightly curled black hair out a bit, but kept it very neat.

"Mrs Hennypeck doesn't get out much." Mr Ivy smiled and leaned forward. "Kenworth, how much further?"

"Almost there, sir. Just around this corner."

The car pulled up, and out climbed the investigators. They stood at the centre of a circular junction in the shadow of an impressively tall stone sundial pillar, and from the circle seven narrow streets broke off, winding away out of sight on all sides. This was Seven Dials, a famous London landmark. Mr Charles Dickens himself had written about the colourful characters that had lived in the Seven Dials area back in the 1800s, the scallywags and street urchins and dregs of society. But as much as the great Mr Dickens knew about London, about its back streets and its alleyways, even he would have been astounded by what happened when Mr Ivy approached the sundial pillar and placed his hand upon the column of stone.

Seven Dials.

Seven streets.

But no…

Look again.

When Mr Ivy removed his hand from the pillar, there were *eight* streets. Another entrance had appeared, narrower than the rest, and smells of roasting chestnuts and paraffin, of cold autumn air and coal smoke, drifted from the entrance. This was the way to Salem Road, London's magic district.

Mr Ivy rushed onwards. "Hurry now."

Mrs Hennypeck bristled. "In case you've forgotten, Mr Ivy, I happen to be deceased."

"It doesn't stop your mouth running, does it?" mumbled Flintwitch.

"What? What was that you said?"

"Oh, nothing…"

Salem Road was cobbled and uneven, lined with jaunty shops and buildings all joined together, with the odd alleyway or court leading into some unseen darkness. The road was a series of twists and turns, and in places it doubled back on itself and then carried on in another direction. Even at this late hour (or early, depending on your viewpoint) there were a handful of shops open, and warm light from their windows fell on the pavement in bars of gold.

The carried on until, at last, they saw a worried-looking woman standing half-in, half-out of a doorway.

"Are you from the Bureau?" she asked.

Mr Ivy took the wallet out of his coat, showed her his badge. "You contacted us?"

"I did," said the woman. "I heard terrible noises through the wall from the flat above old Mr Crane's toy shop next door. Sounded like someone being murdered!"

Mrs Hennypeck frowned. "Crane? You don't mean Neville Crane?"

The woman nodded. "That's right. Know him, do you?"

Mrs Hennypeck shared a dark look with Mr Ivy and Flintwitch. "I did. A long time ago."

Mr Ivy tucked his badge away. "Thank you. Please go back inside now and lock your door. I'm sure there's nothing untoward going on, but you can never be too careful."

The woman took one last snooping glance around and slipped back into her house. Moments later the curtains in an upstairs room began to twitch.

Mrs Hennypeck looked up at the sign above the door.

CRANE'S
TOY MAKERS

EST. 1774

"So Neville ended up back in the family business. He was a good investigator in his day, you know. I watched him grow from a nervous apprentice to a fine magician." She moved to the door, pressed her hand against it, and it clicked open to reveal a darkened room beyond. "Come along. If I know Neville, he'll have put up a fight."

The entrance led them along a hallway, all shadow and creaking boards, and through a door to a workshop filled with woodworking tools. The air was thick with the smell of burning wood and sap, and piles of sawdust blew around on the floor like drifts of snow.

"No sign of a struggle," said Mr Ivy. He reached into his coat pocket, brought out a small book bound in black leather, opened the pages and read a short spell. A ball of warm yellow light floated up from the pages and hung in the air over their heads, lighting the workshop.

Everywhere, hanging from the ceiling, piled on the benches, sat on shelves all around, were wooden puppets, hundreds of them, in various stages of completion.

Young Flintwitch seemed quite enchanted, as did Mr Ivy. Even Mrs Hennypeck took her time wandering around, touching various creations.

"I had one just like this when I was a boy," mused Mr Ivy.

"I did too," said Flintwitch. 'I mean, when I was a *younger* boy."

Mr Ivy led the way through the workshop and up a set of stairs to a small flat on the second floor. There, in the living room, was the victim. Or rather, what was left of the victim.

Mr Ivy stared around the room, and then at the shadows on the floor. There were four people, including himself. But there were five shadows.

The extra shadow had belonged to Neville Crane.

"You feel that?" Mr Ivy held out a hand as if checking for rain.

Mrs Hennypeck nodded. "The air is crackling, isn't it? Positively bursting with energy."

"Another retired Magical Investigator gone," noted Flintwitch. "But why?"

"And how?" added Mr Ivy. "I've never encountered anything capable of vanishing a person out of existence, leaving only a shadow behind."

Mrs Hennypeck stared down at the shadow on the floor, folded her arms and shook her head.

"There's something familiar... something I'm not remembering. Oh, curse this dead old brain of mine!"

Of the three Magical Investigators in attendance, young Flintwitch had the keenest eyes, and now he went creeping towards the shadow on the floor.

"I think... I think there's something in there."

The others joined him and peered into it.

"If you look at it a certain way," Mr Ivy fiddled with the crimson silk scarf around his neck, "it appears to be a—"

"A hole." Mrs Hennypeck's dead little face was full of curiosity, her blue lips pursed in concentration. "A hole in the world."

"It goes down a *looong* way." Flintwitch peered in.

Mr Ivy frowned. "How curious. We have visited four other scenes of this nature, and yet none of the shadows left in those places were like this one. Why do you think that is?"

Mrs Hennypeck's eyes grew suddenly wide. "I know. I know the answer to that. Of course!"

"What? What is it?"

"Don't be alarmed, but the reason that the other shadows weren't like this one is that, in those cases, the creature was no longer at the scene."

Her words hung in the air. Mr Ivy pointed to the shadow. "But... so you're saying... you're not *saying*..."

"It's still here," said Mrs Hennypeck.

And as she spoke those words, something climbed out of the shadow.

CHAPTER 22

FROM THE SHADOWS

Salem Road, London, 1967

The creature, whatever it was, would have been easy to miss had Mr Ivy and his colleagues not been staring so intently at it. It was almost invisible, as if it was made from the clearest glass, only catching the light here or there, bending and warping it. There were hints of familiar forms – a torso perhaps, arms and legs and a head – but every time they thought they saw something, the light would change and shift, and it would be gone again.

Mrs Hennypeck took a step towards the flickering shape, her head tilted to one side, her dead little eyes crunched up in concentration, sparking with the tiniest flicker of recognition.

Mr Ivy reached into his coat, pulled out his leatherbound little book. He opened it with shaking fingers, began to read a binding enchantment…

"Mr Ivy! Look!"

Mr Ivy's shadow had begun to move, to change shape and rise up. He dropped his book on the floor. But nobody can escape their own shadow. As it billowed around him, swallowing him up, Mr Ivy's shadow made a dry, crisp sound, like the winter wind in the branches of a dead tree.

There were cries from the other magicians as their own shadows reared up too, surrounding them, cloaking them in dark shapes. Each of them was experiencing a vision.

"I'm not ready!" screamed Mrs Hennypeck. She lay on her back, banging her fist and scratching the floor as if she was trapped in a box, a coffin. "Let me stay!"

Mr Ivy dropped to his knees and began to beg some invisible force. "Please. Don't take my magic away. I can't go back… I won't!"

Flintwitch was seeing something different again; the way he held his arms suggested he was cradling someone small. Tears were streaming down his face. "Don't take her. Please don't take her. Let her get better…"

Suddenly, he seemed to find strength from deep

within his chest and pushed back against the vision, trembling with the effort of it. "It's not real!" he yelled to the others. "Mr Ivy! Mrs Hennypeck! It's making you see these things!"

He reached inside his coat, brought out a smooth, polished length of hazel wood and stabbed it at his shadow. A terrible sound filled the room, like the scream of something in great pain. Flintwitch's shadow fell back, became his own once more. He dashed to Mr Ivy, swiped the hazel wand at his billowing shadow and pulled him out of the vision. He did the same to Mrs Hennypeck.

Once they were free, Flintwitch touched the tip of his wand to the floor and began to trace a protective circle around the group. He had almost succeeded, almost closed the circle, when the glassy, shimmering creature shot something through the air, a bullet of shadow that plunged deep into Flintwitch's stomach.

He collapsed.

Mr Ivy quickly took the crimson scarf from around his neck and swung it around, flicking the tip of it, whip-like, at this strange creature. When the tip of the scarf snapped in the air, there was a loud crack and a wave of magic swept through the room.

The creature fell back, made that sound again – a sound full of fury and great sadness at the same time. It spun around, smashed through the window and vanished.

Mrs Hennypeck made a dash for the broken window and stared down the quiet street. "It's gone, I think."

"Mrs Hennypeck! Here! Help me!"

Mr Ivy was crouched over Flintwitch's crumpled little body. Flintwitch was writhing and gasping, breathing in ragged, painful gulps.

"Look! His stomach!"

A dark patch of inky liquid was beginning to soak through his waistcoat. Mrs Hennypeck ripped it open and unbuttoned the white shirt, which was quickly turning black too. On Flintwitch's belly was a small circular wound from which viscous black liquid was welling and overflowing. The flesh around the wound was blackening too, spreading outwards.

"He's becoming a shadow'" cried Mr Ivy. "I don't know what to do, Mrs Hennypeck. What if we lose him? He's only a child!"

"Now, you listen here, boy," Mrs Hennypeck said sternly, which captured Mr Ivy's full attention, for he had not been called 'boy' in a very long time. "We're not losing anybody. I know someone who can help. But we must be quick. Whatever this is, it's moving fast."

CHAPTER 23

ECHOES

The Nowhere Emporium, London, Present Day

In the shopfront, Daniel tried to breathe, tried to calm his heart, and when his mind had cleared a little he searched the Emporium with his thoughts and feelings.

"Edna's gone. She left the Emporium, went outside."

"That's not good, Daniel," said Ellie. "She's out of control. It's bad enough she stole the Emporium and caused so much damage, but out there she could kill someone."

Daniel sat at his desk, rubbed his temples. "I just can't believe this is the same girl we met yesterday. It doesn't seem like the same person, you know?"

"So what are you saying? It's not Edna?"

"I'm not sure. I don't think it's as simple as that. I think there's something else going on. We need to find her and bring her back here. For her own good, and to keep the people of London safe."

Ellie went to the window, stared out at the night. Heavy rain had begun to fall and puddles were gathering on the street. "How are we going to find her? London is a big place."

Daniel glanced down at his desk where the *Book of Wonders* lay. Smells of hot butter and summer grass drifted through the red curtain from the Carnival of Wonders beyond. An idea burned bright in his head. Ellie's father had left an echo of his knowledge in the pages of the *Book of Wonders*. *I could ask Mr Silver*, he thought. The magic should work now that they were back in the Emporium, not like when they'd tried in Keswick. But not in front of Ellie. The loss of Mr Silver was still a raw wound.

"You have to do it." Ellie was watching Daniel, and his eyes darted from the book to her.

"Do what?"

"Come off it, Daniel. I know you better than that. I know what you're thinking. And I think you're right. We have to ask him."

"Ellie… we don't have to. There are other ways."

"Like what? We need to get to Edna. Fast. You admitted yourself, you're still learning how to do magic inside the Emporium, never mind out there in the world. We need all the help we can get."

Daniel nodded, but there was still a conflict in his brain. "If I do this… if I bring Mr Silver's echo out of the book… you have to remember that it's not really him, Ellie. It's not like having him back."

She nodded sadly. "I know that."

Daniel reached for the book. He opened it, and paused. "You sure?"

Ellie took a breath. "I'm sure."

Daniel flipped through the *Book of Wonders* until he found what he was looking for: a page filled completely with writing so small that it was impossible to read with the naked eye.

"Mr Silver? It's Daniel. I need your help."

A cold breeze whispered around the room, made them shiver. The book jumped out of Daniel's hands and landed face-down on the desk. Then it burst open again and the pages fanned as if an invisible hand was flicking through them at blinding speed. The book fell open at the same page of incredibly small text. The words shifted and moved, and began to break free of the paper, to drift up into the air and to blow around in the cold, unnatural breeze. Then the letters, the words, clustered together in clumps, and the clumps came together making bigger shapes, a hand here, a foot there, until there was a man floating above the desk. And though he was made entirely from black ink, from tiny words and letters, he was recognisable at once.

"Good day," said the inky echo of Mr Lucien Silver. "How may I be of service?"

Daniel shot a glance towards Ellie; he was not surprised to see her standing quite still, her arms by her sides, staring up at the echo of her father with a mixture of wonder and sadness and hunger. Daniel felt ashamed to be putting her through this. He wanted it over with quickly.

He told the echo of Mr Silver all that had happened with the shop, about the thief and the staff turning to stone.

"My staff? Stone? It's an outrage!"

"Exactly," said Daniel. "So how do I turn them back?"

"I beg your pardon?"

"I've tried turning them back, but the *Book of Wonders* didn't work. So what do I do?"

The echo scratched a chin made of tiny, well-formed letters with a finger made of jumbled sentences. "I'm afraid I don't have a clue."

Daniel blinked. "You don't?"

"Not the foggiest," said Silver's echo.

"But…" Daniel was struggling to find the words, feeling very much like the world had gone suddenly quite mad. "But you're Mr Silver! You know *everything* about this place!"

"That I do," said the inky Mr Silver, "but as much as

you wish to believe otherwise, my boy, I am nothing more than an instruction manual. A handsome one, I'll grant you, but an instruction manual just the same. I cannot react to events happening in the here and now, because, quite simply, I am not here."

"But—"

"I cannot answer questions the real Mr Silver did not anticipate, can I? The knowledge he left in the book was the knowledge he thought you may need."

Daniel pondered this. "Alright. How about this: the girl who stole the shop – Edna – has escaped out into London. She's probably very dangerous, to other people and herself. We need to find her very quickly. How do we do that?"

The echo of Mr Silver stroked his inky chin again.

"Let me think… to track her you'll need some sort of material sensitive to dark magic. Iron from a fallen star, perhaps. Or hazel picked at midnight under a full moon. Or a candle made of dragon fat…"

"Wait," said Daniel. "Hazel? Like this?" He still had the hazel wand tucked inside his jacket, the one Arthur had given him before they'd come to London.

"Exactly like that," said the echo.

"So what do we do with it?" asked Ellie. Daniel was surprised to hear her addressing the echo of her dead father; he could see how much it was hurting her to be so close to him and yet so very far away.

The ink Mr Silver showed no fondness for her.

He cleared his throat and began to speak as if reading from a textbook. "Hazel, a deciduous broadleaf tree native to the UK, is well known in certain magical communities for possessing several unique properties. Hazel can be used, for instance, to fuel a fire, which will, if burnt at midnight, allow any magicians present to see visions…"

Daniel made a pushing motion. "Can we hurry this along a bit? How can this help us *tonight?*"

The shadow of Mr Silver shook his head. "Alright, alright! Good lord. Now let me see… Ah, yes. You shall need something belonging to the person you wish to track – an item of clothing perhaps. Do you have that?"

"Why would we have anything she's worn?" asked Ellie.

Daniel snapped his fingers. "Hold on!" He began excitedly rummaging in his pockets, at last bringing out a small piece of broken plastic. "This was hers. It broke off the camera she wore around her neck. Will it work?"

"I daresay it will," said the echo.

"OK, what do we do now?"

"Well, it goes like this: take a sharp knife and strip one end of the hazel stick down to a point. Then take a length of string and tie one end around an object belonging to the person you wish to find – in this case the broken camera piece – and tie the other end around the middle of the hazel stick. Holding the camera piece, let the stick hang in the air. The stick will begin to spin, and the sharpened end will act as a pointer... Are you listening?"

Daniel was not listening. He was already rooting around in the various drawers and compartments of his desk. He brought out a sharp knife and a ball of twine, and he took the knife and carefully sharpened one end of his hazel stick to a point. Then he cut a length of string and tied it around the stick and the broken camera piece.

"Oh, it was no trouble," said the echo of Mr Silver. "You're welcome, I'm sure."

With that, he disappeared back into the pages of the *Book of Wonders* with a pop.

Daniel held the wand up to show Ellie, but stopped. There were tears in her eyes and she was staring at the spot where the echo of her father had appeared.

"Ellie...' He tried to put an arm around her, but she shrugged away.

"It's too much. It's all too much."

"But you said it was OK. I wouldn't have done it..."

"Oh, I'm not blaming you, Daniel. I wouldn't ever want you to think that. It's this place. It's filled with memories." She pointed at the *Book of Wonders*. "Literally filled with ghosts. I can't escape them. Everywhere I look there's something else to remind me of him. I can't go on like this. I have to change things."

Daniel swallowed. "You mean leave?"

She dabbed at her eyes with her knuckles. "We'll talk later. I'm being stupid. Come on, we've work to do. Let's find Edna and get her home."

CHAPTER 24

THE LOST TOWER

London, 1967

The black Rolls Royce Phantom screeched around the corner. Kenworth gunned the engine and headed straight for a chain-link fence that had been erected around an abandoned tower block.

The car mounted the pavement – *bump* – and tore through the fence, rattling over the overgrown wasteground before finally skidding to a stop at the tower block entrance. The back doors of the car flew open, and out jumped Mr Ivy and Mrs Hennypeck. Kenworth hurried out from behind the wheel, rushed around the car, reached in the back and reappeared with young Flintwitch cradled in his arms.

"You sure about this, Mrs Hennypeck?" Mr Ivy stared up at the unfinished building, a tower of bare grey concrete. Many of the floors looked to have been completed, but around the halfway point it seemed that construction had ceased, and above there was only the skeleton of a building, steel beams and unfinished rooms open to the night.

"Just follow me," said Mrs Hennypeck.

The entranceway was open – there was no door – and they walked through to a dark, silent lobby. The floor was half-tiled, and there were still plastic sheets on the ground and tins of paint scattered around. The lift shafts were open and empty, and the wind whistled down them into the lobby.

"This way."

Through a door they went to a narrow stairwell, and began to climb the naked concrete stairs. The air was thick with dust and dampness. A cold night breeze swept down from the openings high above, and the quiet was punctuated by the rasping breathing of Flintwitch, who writhed and twitched in Kenworth's arms.

Up and up they climbed, floor after floor.

"The everyday folk started building this block in the early sixties," said Mrs Hennypeck. "But from day one the job seemed to be cursed. Builders were injured. Tools were lost. There were reports of entire floors rearranging themselves and swapping places.

It got worse and worse, until the owners eventually put construction on hold."

Mr Ivy listened with great interest. "Magicians?"

Mrs Hennypeck nodded.

"Sir," said Kenworth, "Master Flintwitch… I think he's running out of time."

Darkness was creeping out from the wound in Flintwitch's belly, spreading all over his body. It had reached his throat, and his eyes rolled back, and he moaned and shivered. He was becoming a shadow.

"Hang on, Flintwitch," said Mr Ivy. "How much further, Mrs Hennypeck?"

"Almost there. In fact… yes, this is it."

They had come to a stop at the entrance to what Mr Ivy estimated to be the seventh or eighth floor; the door here had been fitted, and he opened it, staring down the dark, lifeless corridor.

"Shut the door!" cried Mrs Hennypeck. "You know better than that!"

He did as she said, and Mrs Hennypeck reached out a cold, dead hand and touched the tip of her finger to the door. She traced a series of shapes, then nodded. "Now you may open it."

This time, when Mr Ivy opened the door, he was no longer met by a dark, lifeless corridor, but by a hallway lit by gas lamps, alive with the sounds of laughter and chatter, and of people living in the flats beyond.

Mrs Hennypeck led the way through a corridor thick with the stench of bubbling potions. Mr Ivy recognised the scents of liquid starlight and firedrops and moon nettle, all dangerous and illegal potion ingredients.

"Why don't I know about this place?" He gave Mrs Hennypeck a sideways glance.

"Not many of us do," she said. "A word of advice: don't show your badge here – it'll probably get you killed."

"Killed? I'm Chief of the Bureau! If there's illegal activity going on I should—"

Mrs Hennypeck stopped and looked at him. "Some secrets are worth keeping. You'll see."

Flintwitch suddenly let out a gurgling cry and became very still. Black, viscous liquid began dripping from his nose and running from the corners of his eyes.

"Hurry! This way!"

Along the corridor, past an open door where they could see into a flat bursting with cauldrons, all belching coloured smoke into the air. A woman tossed something wet and wriggling into one of the cauldrons, and a huge explosion filled the flat, sending a rancid plume of smoke out into the passageway.

They came to the last door, and Mrs Hennypeck banged hard on it with her fist.

Footsteps from the other side.

The sound of locks and chains.

The door opened a crack, and a pair of large brown eyes stared out.

"Mr Pepper. It's me. Mrs Hennypeck."

Mr Pepper opened the door wider, sent a probing glance up the hallway. He was tall and rumpled; if someone decided to get dressed while hanging upside down in the dark in the middle of a hurricane, the results would be similar.

"Mrs Hennypeck," he took her hand and kissed it, "you're looking well."

Mrs Hennypeck did not look impressed. "I'm dead."

"Yes, but oh how it *suits* you."

"We have an emergency, Mr Pepper. Our young friend needs help. Quickly."

Mr Pepper's large brown eyes drifted down towards the boy in Kenworth's arms. "Oh dear," he said, without even a trace of concern. "The poor lad's almost ready to join you."

"We need to see her," said Mrs Hennypeck. "Now."

Mr Pepper held out a hand, palm upwards, expectant.

Mrs Hennypeck rummaged in her coat, brought out a small glass vial with a cork stopper, and handed it over. Mr Pepper took the vial and held it up close to his face so that he might examine the contents. Inside was what at first glance appeared to be a glowing blue liquid. But if you looked close enough, you could see that it was not liquid at all; it was a soup of tiny letters and words, each glowing like a miniature star.

Mr Pepper tucked the vial away in his pocket. "The doctor will see you now."

CHAPTER 25

THE GHOST DOCTOR

London, 1967

In light of Mr Pepper's dishevelled appearance, you might assume that his flat would be an untidy, ramshackle place. This assumption would be incorrect.

The place was spotlessly clean, filled with fine furniture and a smell of varnish. An antique grandfather clock stood in the hallway like a sentry. There were shelves and display cabinets, proudly displaying hundreds of glass vials of various shapes and sizes, containing glowing words of many colours.

Mr Ivy peered closer. "Are those…"

"Dreams," said Mrs Hennypeck. "Possibly the purest form of imagination. He deals in them."

"Bring the boy in here," said Mr Pepper.

The room was small and bare, save for a flat table in the centre with many drawers and compartments. A hook-nosed woman with piercing green eyes stared out from an oil painting on the wall.

"Lay him down. That's it."

Kenworth put Flintwitch on the table. He was still and his breathing was shallow. The shadow had almost completely taken him.

"He's slipping away," said Mr Ivy.

"Yes, yes. Give me a moment. Leave it to the experts…"

Mr Pepper crouched down, opened up one of the drawers in the table and brought out a black candle with a black wick. There was an ornate silver candlestick on a sideboard beneath the oil painting, and Mr Pepper placed the black candle on the candlestick and lit it.

The flame was black, as was the smoke, and as it drifted upwards towards the painting, something amazing happened. Some of the smoke was drawn into the painting, into the woman's mouth and nose, as if she was breathing it in. And then she started to move, to breathe and blink and look around. Her gaze rested on poor Flintwitch on the table. Then she turned her head towards Mrs Hennypeck.

"Bronwyn? Bronwyn Hennypeck?"

"Yes, ma'am," Mrs Hennypeck's reply caused Mr Ivy and Kenworth to raise their eyebrows and exchange a look of some amazement, for Mrs Hennypeck had never before, as far as they could recollect, referred to anyone as 'ma'am'. "We've brought you a boy, ma'am. Injured in the line of duty. His injuries are, I think, beyond the reach of anyone but you. Can you help him, ma'am?"

"Very well," replied the woman. "I'll need a closer look."

From the painting, into the room, came a coil of glowing silver smoke. The smoke drifted over the table, over Flintwitch's body, and then into the wound. A few moments later the coil of smoke reappeared, and swirled and tumbled, and took the shape of the woman in the painting, until she was there with them in the room, a ghost made of soft silvery light.

"Incredible." Mr Ivy's tone was hushed and reverent. "I have read, of course, about the possibility of storing one's soul in a painting, but I have never seen it in action—"

"Quiet," instructed the ghostly woman. She began to examine Flintwitch. More and more of him had been overtaken by shadow; the effect was rather like looking at a picture on an old television set. Flintwitch flickered and was, it seemed, substantial one moment and made from shadows the next. "You were right to

166

bring him here. No medicine from the world of the living could fix this…" She reached an ethereal hand into the wound and felt around. Flintwitch moaned. "I'm sorry," said the ghostly woman. "It'll be over soon… There… Got it!"

The hand made of light gently retracted from the wound, and between her fingers the woman held a long, black creature, a writhing ribbon of shadow. It curled and spat and thrashed. "The bottom drawer on that side," said the woman. "Get me a jar!"

Mr Ivy hurriedly did as she asked, and unscrewed the heavy lid. The ghost dropped the creature into the jar, and Mr Ivy screwed the lid shut.

"Now the next drawer up. That's it. Fetch me a bottle from there. No, not that one… one of the slender green ones. That's it. Now pour a few drops into his mouth and a splash or two into the wound."

Again Mr Ivy followed her instructions. The wound steamed and hissed and closed up, and almost at once the shadow began to recede, until Flintwitch looked whole once more.

"I think I got it all," said the ghost. "When he wakes he should be fine. You were fortunate to get here when you did. A few more minutes and he would have been beyond even my help."

"How long will he sleep?" asked Mrs Hennypeck.

"Perhaps a few hours. Perhaps a few minutes. Everyone is different." She looked down at the candle.

"Almost burned away already. I don't have much time left, but I am curious. What caused his injury?"

They explained everything, about the attacks and the shadows and the strange creature that was prowling London, attacking former Bureau investigators.

"Tell me those names again," said the ghost, "the ones who have been attacked."

Mr Ivy repeated the names.

The ghost listened intently, seeming to roll the names around in her head. Then her eyes stretched wide.

"The Needle Incident!"

Mr Ivy looked around the room. Nobody said anything. "What does that mean?" he whispered to Mrs Hennypeck, who looked blankly back at him.

"Don't you remember, Bronwyn?" asked the ghost. "It happened just before I retired from the Bureau."

"Hold on," said Mr Ivy. "You mean to say *you* were in the Bureau?"

The ghost stared at him. 'Bronwyn, who is this… person?"

"Mr Ivy, ma'am. The current Chief."

The ghost looked Mr Ivy up and down. "We have let our standards slip, haven't we?"

Mr Ivy looked scandalised. "I beg your pardon, madam!" But he stopped, because a realisation had struck him like a hammer. "Those green eyes. I knew

I'd seen them before. There's a portrait of you in my office at Number 120 Park Street. Only, in that painting you are younger and very much…"

"Alive?"

"Yes! But if you have a portrait in Park Street, that would mean you're a former Chief."

"Well done, boy. You got there in the end. Agatha Wimple's the name. And yes – your office once belonged to me."

Mr Ivy gave a small bow. "Incredible."

"Ma'am," said Mrs Hennypeck, "since I died, I've found that my memory is not what it was. The Needle Incident… remind me."

"There was a creature loose in London," said Agatha Wimple. "Not your run-of-the-mill ghost or vampire, but a Shade Walker – a magician who had become so immensely powerful with dark magic that shadow had swallowed him up and he had transformed into something else: a creature able to flit between worlds, to shapeshift, to drink the magic and life force of other magicians. I sent seven of my best investigators after the Shade Walker. And one of them is in this room."

Everyone looked at Mrs Hennypeck, but she did not see them. She was staring far off into the past.

"I *remember*. We tracked it down, cornered it. Fighting it was like fighting all the darkness in the world. It made us see visions… terrible things. Bob

Needle – an investigator – got too close. The dark wrapped around him, turned him to shadow, and then he was gone, vanished away to nothing. We destroyed the Shade Walker. When it was over we searched for Bob, but we couldn't find any trace of him."

"So," said Mr Ivy, "we have another Shade Walker on the loose?"

Mrs Hennypeck's dead little eyes alighted on Mr Ivy. "I knew I was missing something. Six of us fought the Shade Walker and came back alive, Mr Ivy. The attacks we've been investigating these past days, the magicians who've been turned to shadow – they are the survivors of that night."

"But you destroyed the Shade Walker," said Mr Ivy.

"We certainly thought so... but this *has* to be the same one. It's back, and it's going after all the investigators who fought it that night. Five of the six are no longer with us. And that can mean only one thing: I'm next."

The candle flickered again, began to fizz.

"My time's up," said the ghost of Agatha Wimple. "Retrace your steps, Bronwyn. Use the past to help you..." She flickered and faded, disappearing for a moment before blinking back into sight. "Filigree & Son. The old department store. Where you fought him the first time..."

She faded and blinked out again, and this time she did not come back.

Mr Ivy and Mrs Hennypeck stared at the portrait on the wall where Agatha Wimple was now still and peaceful.

Then there was a rustle from the table.

Flintwitch sat up, and yawned, and looked about.

"Have I missed anything?

Shortly thereafter, as the investigators prepared to once more head into the night, Mr Ivy slipped into an empty room, closed the door and pulled a piece of paper and a pen from his coat. He wrote a hurried message on the paper, and when he was done he read and reread it several times, wondering if he was doing the right thing. But the situation was dire, was it not? Lives were on the line. Desperate times and all that…

He walked over to the window, took a deep breath and recited a spell, his lips curling around every syllable. While he spoke, the piece of paper in his hands burst into flame. As the paper burned, the letters on the page began to glow, and while the paper turned to ash, the letters of the message remained, floating, white-hot, in the air. When all the paper was gone, Mr Ivy stared at the words he'd written. Then he opened the window and, with a flick of his hand, the letters swirled around the room then flew out into the dark.

"It's done now," said Mr Ivy to himself. "No going back."

As the message flew, it passed through the world we know, through the borders of time and space, through the door between everything and nothing. The message itself was simple, but its journey was not. Because it was looking for an address that was ever-changing and for a man who did not wish to be found:

Mr Lucien Silver
The Nowhere Emporium

CHAPTER 26

FACING THE PAST

London, Present Day

"G'night, Mr Ivy! Come again soon. Here, let me get that door for you."

"No, it's fine, Bill, it's fine. I'm not so old I can't manage just yet. Goodnight."

Mr Ivy left the warmth of the pub and stopped in the doorway, glaring at the battering raindrops. He tossed the old crimson silk scarf around his neck, and as he began to hobble up the street, leaning heavily with his free hand on a wooden walking stick, the raindrops bent around him, leaving him dry.

When Mr Ivy went out to drink, which was not very often these days, he liked to leave the magic district. If he went to a pub on Salem Road, someone would recognise him from his days in the Bureau and he'd be expected to tell stories of his great adventures. Out in the everyday world, nobody bothered him.

On the walk home to Seven Dials he decided to take a slightly longer route, cutting along Park Street. He stopped across the road from Number 120 and stared at the front door.

If I walk up and knock on that door, he thought, *I will find the inside just as I left it the day I retired. Kenworth will still be there, of course. It would be good to catch up. And I should like to see my portrait hanging in the Chief's office.* He almost stepped off the pavement, but he stopped himself. *I'm tired, and I've had too much to drink. Nobody from the Bureau wants an old fool like me chapping on the door at this hour. I should get home to bed.*

The magic district was almost deserted when he got there; it was the middle of the night, though a select few pubs and shops stayed open right through until morning – namely those in which black market dealings took place. Twenty years ago, before he retired from the Bureau, Mr Ivy would have been very interested in that sort of thing, keen to shut it all down. But the world was a different place now. Magic wasn't what it once was, and neither, unfortunately, was Mr Ivy.

He turned the corner and stopped in the doorway of his home. He rummaged in his pocket for his keys, unlocked the door with stiff old fingers and let himself in. He shook the water from his umbrella, took off his coat and hung it up on the coat stand by the door. Shivering, he turned to close the front door to the driving rain.

"Hello."

A girl stood out on the street a few paces back from the doorway. She was tall and she wore thick glasses, the rain sliding down the smudged lenses.

"Hello," said Mr Ivy. "You'd better go home, young lady. You'll catch your death."

She took a single step towards him, and he caught proper sight of her in the light spilling from his home. When he saw her shadow – the shadow of a man, not a young girl – the breath caught in his tired old chest.

He nodded once. It was a tired nod. A nod of resignation.

"I know what you are," he said. "I'll never forget the feeling of being around you all those years ago. The feeling of dread and fear." He stared into the girl's eyes, knowing that he was not really talking to a young girl at all, but something dark and ancient and powerful that had taken her prisoner. "I assume you're going to kill me? You won't have any trouble this time, I imagine. I'm old, and weak, and alone. But at least let me go inside and have one last drink, eh? Let me die in the comfort of my own home?"

The girl nodded.

Mr Ivy turned and hobbled through the house. He heard her shutting the front door, heard the rain fading to the background, heard her footsteps follow him into the comfortable sitting room. He poured himself a drink, and sat in his favourite chair, and listened to the sound of the ice in his glass.

The girl did not sit. She stood in the centre of the room, rain dripping from her clothes and her hair and the end of her nose, and she stared at him.

"Please let the girl go," he said. "Use my shadow instead. She doesn't deserve this."

The girl's shadow, the shadow that was shaped like a man, spoke in a voice as old and dry as a dead autumn leaf. "Why would I want you? You said it yourself – you are old and weak, like the others I've killed. The girl is young and strong. I think I'll stay where I am. Soon I won't need to use another's shadow in any case."

Mr Ivy searched the girl's eyes. "Are you still in there? Can you hear me?"

The shadow became agitated. "She's gone!"

"No. I don't believe that." Mr Ivy looked up into the girl's eyes again. "What's your name? Can you tell me that? Do you remember?" As he watched the girl's eyes, he saw a flicker of light there, of life. "That's it.

Fight it. Think of the people you love, the places you feel warm and comfortable and safe. Hold on to those feelings. Now, what's your name?"

The girl was shaking with effort, and beads of sweat were mixing with the rain on her skin. "Ed-Ed-Edna." Her voice was so weak it almost wasn't there.

Mr Ivy climbed from his seat, took her hands. "That's it, Edna. Fight! Push back!"

"I've done something bad," whispered Edna. "I can't go back. I'll get in terrible trouble…"

The man in Edna's shadow reared up, and a great blast of energy knocked Mr Ivy back into his armchair. When he next looked up at Edna, she was staring at the floor, unable and unwilling to meet his gaze.

"Where is the old lady?" asked the shadow. "Where is the walking corpse who wears the necklace?"

Mr Ivy put his drink down on the coffee table. He knew at once the reason this creature wanted Mrs Hennypeck. Her necklace.

He reached into his pocket and pulled out his crimson silk scarf. "It's beautiful, isn't it?" He held the scarf close to his face. "It was a gift from my dear wife, many years ago. I don't suppose I'll be needing it any more, will I? Not where I'm going." He balled up the scarf and tossed it into the fire, and it burned in a brilliant flash of light and became dust.

"Where is the dead woman?" the shadow repeated.

Mr Ivy took another sip of his drink. "I don't know."

"You'll tell me in the end."

Mr Ivy finished his drink. "I might." He stood up, managing for the first time in many years to stand straight and tall. "Let's see, shall we?"

This time his eyes were drawn to his own shadow, and he saw it shift and grow and move, saw it rise up from the floor. As his shadow swallowed him, Mr Ivy's thoughts turned back many years, to those terrible shadows he'd discovered on his investigations, and he knew that he was going to experience what those poor people had gone through, that his last moments would be identical to theirs.

He closed his eyes.

And then it began.

CHAPTER 27

FINDING EDNA

London, Present Day

"It's not working!"

"You sure you're holding it right?"

"Ellie, how many ways can there be of dangling a stick from a bit of string?"

"Well, I don't know how this works, do I?"

The two of them stood in their raincoats peering down at the hazel stick on the end of the string, rain falling so hard around them that it bounced as it hit the pavement. Miniature rivers at the edge of the roads coursed into overworked drains.

The stick wasn't moving. Daniel gave it a flick, and it spun in lazy circles and came to a stop in exactly the same position. There was no sign at all that the wand was picking anything up.

"Give it here," said Ellie. "You sure it's tied properly?" She took the string from Daniel, and as soon as her fingers touched it, a spark shot from the end of the twig and it began to twirl.

"How'd you get it to do that?"

"I don't know. I didn't do anything!"

They waited and watched, and the stick spun faster and faster, until it was a blur in the rain. Then, suddenly, it stopped, the sharp end pointing off across the road in an entirely new direction. Daniel looked up at Ellie, who was smiling in stunned amazement.

"I've never done anything magic before!" She tried to hand the wand on the string back to him, but he backed away.

"No. You hold on to it. It's working for you."

They began to hurry in the direction that the stick indicated, and as they moved it swung gently, pointing towards some unknown force the way a compass points north. On they went, along another road, this one quite narrow, and out into a circular junction with seven roads leading off it and a tall stone sundial standing in the centre.

"I know where we are," said Daniel. "It's Salem Road!"

Ellie looked at him blankly, blinking rain from her eyes.

"Are you kidding me?" said Daniel. "You've never heard of Salem Road? Your dad must've come here hundreds of times! I had a trip here not long after I took over the Emporium. Don't you remember me going on and on about it?"

Ellie shrugged. "To be honest, Daniel, I don't listen to a lot of the guff that falls out of your mouth. Oh, don't take it personally – it was the same with Papa. I'm just not interested in any of that technical magical history-type stuff. I'm more of a wing-it-and-let's-see-what-happens type of person, you know?"

"Right," said Daniel, feeling more than a little affronted on behalf of magicians everywhere. "OK. As I was saying – and don't worry, I'll try not to bore you too much – Salem Road is the magic district here in London. It's one of the biggest in the world. A lot of it's empty now, but it's still the capital of British magic. And the way in is…" He went to the stone sundial pillar in the centre of the circular street. The pillar reached up towards the dark sky from a large, square base. Daniel walked around it once, and then placed his hand on the stone facade of one of the base's sides. He stood up and smiled, and pointed over Ellie's shoulder.

The entrance to an *eighth* street had appeared.

The hazel wand turned and pointed towards Salem Road.

"In we go, I guess," said Ellie.

Salem Road was mostly quiet at this late hour, and the few magicians they did pass seemed too occupied in their own affairs to even raise an eyebrow at the sight of two children following a spinning hazel wand on a bit of string. In fact, those they passed in the cobbled street were, if anything, up to even stranger business than Daniel and Ellie.

One woman struggled past, a sack slung over her shoulder. There were things moving inside it, and strange slime had soaked through the material and was dripping on the road, hissing and spitting as the rain fell upon it. Another magician, a young man in a wide-brimmed hat, was laughing hysterically at a seemingly invisible companion, slapping this invisible person on what Daniel presumed was the back.

"Oh, good form!" he was yelling between great bellowing laughs. "Oh, you are a hoot!"

Ellie stared after him and said, "I'm beginning to think that Papa might have actually been one of the more stable magicians around…"

The rain showed no sign of letting up; if anything it was falling heavier than ever, spraying back towards the sky as it hit the ground, forming a thin mist that hung in the eerie yellow lamplight of London's magic district.

The hazel wand spun suddenly to the left, pointing to the door of a comfortable-looking house. A single light was on in one of the front rooms.

"The door's open a little," said Ellie in a hushed voice. "You think Edna's here?"

Daniel stared hard at the front door of the house. "I think we're about to find out." He tried to sound brave, but he couldn't hide the waver in his voice. "Together?"

Ellie gave him a nod, and to his great surprise she took his hand. "Together."

They reached up at the same time and pushed on the door.

Through the falling rain, two sounds came from the house. First a smash, like a vase or glass shattering. And then an echoing scream.

Daniel's heart almost jumped into his throat. Without thinking properly about what he was doing, he pushed through into the hallway. The house was in dark silence. At the end of the hallway, a door was lying open, and light from the room cast a hazy bar of gold out onto the floor and the wall.

Standing in this light was Edna.

It was obvious that something was very wrong with her.

Her face was gaunt, her flesh waxy and slick with sweat. Her eyes were blank, devoid of emotion. And then Daniel looked at her shadow, and he saw that it was not her shadow at all. It was the shadow of a man.

"Edna. It's me, Daniel. You remember? From the Nowhere Emporium."

Edna stared straight ahead. But her shadow – the shadow shaped like a tall man in a hat – moved, then pointed towards Daniel and Ellie.

At once Daniel's chest became tight, his heart cold and weak, and his own shadow broke away from the floor, growing and billowing around him, locking him in a dark fog.

Somewhere, he heard Ellie call his name. "Daniel!"

It seemed he was back in the dormitory of St Catherine's Children's Home, the cold, forbidding building where he'd lived before Mr Silver had helped him escape to the world of magic. He felt the sterile air, smelled the too-clean tang of bleach and choking air-freshener.

Spud Harper was there too, the bully who'd made Daniel's life miserable, and his gang, standing all around him. Spud smiled down maliciously. "It was all a dream, Danny boy. None of it was real. This is your future. You're nobody. No pals. No magic. No way out."

"No," cried Daniel. "No!"

They began to laugh at him.

He was shaking badly, shivering with panic. What if they were right? What if he'd dreamed the whole thing, the Emporium and Mr Silver and the world of magic? Every passing moment was dragging him further away from the world, into a never-ending darkness.

Then Ellie's voice broke through. The sound of it warmed him, made him wake up, and suddenly she was beside him, standing with him in his own nightmare as Spud and the gang pointed and laughed and yelled names at him. Ellie took Daniel's hand, and she touched the tip of the hazel wand to the floor and traced a circle around their feet. At once the vision of the orphanage, of Spud and his cronies, turned to ash, and Daniel's shadow shrunk back and became his own once more.

The man in Edna's shadow yelled out and sent a great shockwave down the hall, knocking Daniel and Ellie to the ground. They scrambled up, spun around, braced for another attack, but found the hallway empty. There was no sign of Edna or her shadow, and the only sound was their own breathless gasping.

A distant, ghostly moaning sound drifted from the open door up the hallway, and they ran to the door, bursting into the room. The sitting room was comfortable, decorated in warm golds and deep reds. A fire was burning well.

On the floor was a shadow.

Wait.

No.

Not just a shadow.

The shadow of a man who wasn't there; it was as if he was standing in the room and the light was hitting him and casting the shadow on the floor. The shadow was flickering, and as Daniel crept towards it, he gasped at what he saw. "There's someone in there!"

It was a frightening vision: the face of an old man in the shadow, barely visible, staring up at them.

"He's saying something," said Ellie, moving closer.

The old man's face flickered. His eyes were wide and his mouth moving, screaming something they couldn't quite make out.

"We have to help him!"

"How?"

Daniel bent down, reached into the shadow; it was cold as ice water, and he brought his hand out again quickly, shook the feeling back into his fingers.

A weak, echoing voice drifted out of the shadow. "Please…" The man strobed in and out of view, and his features blurred and darkened at the edges.

"How can we help?" Daniel asked. "How can we get you out?"

"No," said the old man in the shadow. "Not me. Too late…" He faded again, and it seemed that every time he came back more of him was shadow than before. "Mrs He-He-Hennypeck. Help her. It's after her necklace. You must—"

His eyes grew wider and a look of great fear contorted his features as he seemed to fall down, down, down into the shadow. This time he did not come back.

Daniel touched the shadow on the floor, the impossible shadow, and it was no longer cold. "He's gone."

Ellie covered her mouth in shock. "What is this, Daniel? How can someone just become a shadow like that?"

Daniel was unable to tear his gaze from the floor. "Edna's in real trouble, Ellie." The feeling of helplessness was rising in his chest. "I don't know what to do…"

"Don't move! Not an inch!"

This new voice gave Daniel and Ellie a jolt, and they each spun around and raised their hazel wands.

There was a man in the room. He had ebony skin and a crop of neat black hair, and he was dressed in a smart suit and long coat and gloves. His piercing green eyes were alert and intelligent, and they scanned the room from Daniel to Ellie and finally to the shadow on the floor. His mouth dropped open, and he took a step towards Daniel.

"You! What happened?"

"Whoa! Back off! We're not the bad guys here!"

The man reached into his coat, brought out a wallet and opened it, showing them an official-looking silver badge.

"Grover Flintwitch, Chief of the Bureau of Magical Investigation."

Daniel screwed up his face. "The Bureau? What's going on here?"

"I'm the one with the badge, boy, so I'll ask the questions. Who are you?"

"Daniel Holmes. Look, we came here because we're trying to help someone. A girl… It sounds crazy, but there's something living in her shadow. We think it's controlling her. We found her here but she had already attacked the man who lives here. " Daniel pointed to the shadow on the floor.

Mr Flintwitch looked torn between anger and fear. He took a little black leather-bound book from his pocket. The sight of it immediately reminded Daniel of the *Book of Wonders*. Mr Flintwitch opened it, read a passage under his breath, and Daniel felt a warm sensation washing over him, like the tongue of some giant creature had licked him from head to foot.

Mr Flintwitch gave both Daniel and Ellie a final, appraising look. Seemingly satisfied, he snapped the book shut and approached the shadow on the floor.

"What was that? What did you just do?"

"Made sure you were telling the truth," said the man. He began to examine the shadow on the floor.

"When we got here he was still in there," said Ellie. "Inside his own shadow. He said something to us before he disappeared."

"Mr Ivy? What did he say? Please try to remember exactly." The man looked up at Ellie, and she couldn't help but recognise the look in his eyes, the look of grief.

"He said it was too late to save him," said Ellie softly. "And then he asked us to save someone else… Mrs Hen… Henny-something."

Mr Flintwitch made in involuntary movement; his hand went to his chest, pressed against his heart. "Hennypeck?"

"Yes! That's it! He said this shadow thing is after a necklace."

Mr Flintwitch's arms dropped to his sides. He began to look all about, and Daniel could almost hear the spark and fizz of his mind working.

"I must go. I only hope I can get there in time. You two – with me. There are more questions I want to ask." He turned and dashed for the door, into the rain-soaked night.

Daniel and Ellie followed close at his heels.

"Hey! Wait!" said Daniel. "What'll happen to Edna? The girl? She hasn't done anything wrong. Will she be hurt?"

"Honestly?" replied Mr Flintwitch, "I don't know."

CHAPTER 28

THE LAIR

London, 1967

At one time, Filigree & Son had been the grandest, most exclusive department store in all of London. Now, as Mr Ivy and his friends stood in the deserted darkness of the main atrium, staring up and around at the overlooking floors, it was nothing more than a shell, the bare bones of a once-great creature.

"I remember when this place opened," said Mrs Hennypeck, glancing sadly around. "Why, Queen Victoria herself cut the ribbon. For many years this was the place to be seen in the eyes of everyone who was anyone." She recited a light spell, and a glowing orb appeared in the air above their heads, casting the place in cold, pale light. "Look at it now, eh?"

Many of the shelving units still remained, empty and dust-smothered, and the floor was littered with fallen signs and banners:

CLOSING DOWN SALE! EVERYTHING MUST GO!

Somehow it felt colder in the abandoned store than it had out on the London streets, and the air was infused with the smell of stale perfume and damp, rotting wood. Beyond the glow of the light, the shop faded to thick gloom. There were shapes in the darkness, shapes that might have been shadows and might have been something else.

They walked slowly; it was a rambling old maze of a place, with twists and turns and steps, and the dark made it seem cavernous, made their footsteps echo on the rotting floorboards.

"I can feel it," said Mr Ivy quietly, "smell it, the atmosphere... It's like fear's been painted on everything, contaminating the very air."

"It's getting colder," added Flintwitch.

Mrs Hennypeck, who did not have to concern herself with such inconveniences as breathing or the cold, nodded. "I feel it too, in my own way. Something is definitely off."

They made their way up a dormant escalator to the first floor, which had been the gents' clothing department. It was filled with mannequins and empty racks and peeling posters on the walls featuring models with perfect teeth and hair, smiling blankly into the empty darkness.

"Did you hear that?" Flintwitch raised a finger. "Something creaking somewhere?"

But Mr Ivy was not paying him any attention. He was too busy staring into the gloom. "There! Look!"

There were things moving in the shadows all around, lumbering shapes closing in.

Mrs Hennypeck's light spell stopped working. They were plunged into complete darkness.

"What's happening?"

"I don't know! I can't get it going again!"

"I'm trying too. It's not working!"

"What was that sound?"

"Listen, it's coming from over here, behind me."

"No. It's this way!"

Mrs Hennypeck's light spell blazed back to life just long enough for the magicians to glimpse dozens of lumbering, faceless bodies moving towards them.

"It's the mannequins!" cried Mrs Hennypeck. "The Shade Walker is using the mannequins against us!"

Her light spell burned again and they saw that the mannequins were closer now. Mr Ivy raised a hand, ripping one of the dummies apart by the power of his spell. But the pieces pulled back together, re-formed, and the faceless mannequin stood up and came at them again.

"Stay close! With me!" Mr Ivy shouted.

They formed a circle, back to back, and as the light came and went, flash after flash like lightning, they each cast spells, throwing mannequins across the store, ripping them to pieces.

"They just keep coming!" yelled Flintwitch, making a jerking motion with his hands, scattering one of the mannequins far across the room. "There are too many!"

Mr Ivy stepped forwards. He closed his eyes, gathered as much power as he could and unleashed a shockwave of energy that ripped through the store, reducing the mannequins to piles of ash where they stood. Drained from the effort, he dropped to his knees and slumped on the floor. The others rushed to his side.

"I'll be fine. Just need a minute to recover."

But there was no time for that.

"Our shadows!" said Flintwitch. "Look!" Their shadows were moving, growing, morphing into billows of black cloud. "It's the Shade Walker," he said. "It's here!"

Mr Ivy struggled to his feet. "Mrs Hennypeck!

The light spell! Extinguish it, quick! We can't cast shadows without light."

"I'm trying," she cried. "It won't go out!"

The shadows reared up and swirled at each of the investigators, engulfing them in nightmares and fear.

Cocooned in her shadow, Mrs Hennypeck was suddenly inside a coffin, being lowered into the ground. She found that she could not move, that even as she was screaming in her head, no sound was escaping her mouth. The coffin bumped to a stop. Then she heard the sound of dirt hitting the lid. *They're going to bury me! I'm not ready! I'm still here!*

Mrs Hennypeck started awake as the terrible vision faded. Her shadow rolled back just enough that she could see out into the dark department store. And there it was, moving towards her: the Shade Walker.

She could not move as it approached, translucent, the edges of it catching the light here and there, hinting at familiar shapes. It stopped beside her and she saw, unmistakably, a man's hand. It reached out, the edge of its fingers refracting the light, and she knew. She knew that it was going to rip off her necklace, to take its revenge on the last surviving magician from that fateful night.

She tried to shout out, tried to fight, but her shadow held her tight, and as the hand came closer she knew that this was how it finally ended for Bronwyn Hennypeck. The necklace was all that was keeping her whole, anchoring her soul to her body. Without it she would move on to the next life, and to the mysteries that awaited her there. As the hand reached her necklace, Mrs Hennypeck closed her eyes.

Then came the sound of smashing glass and the crowing call of a bird in the darkness.

A glinting shape swooped down through the atrium, a bird. A silver magpie circling overhead. Mrs Hennypeck felt a great crackling power radiating from the bird, spreading out through the store with every beat of its wings.

The Shade Walker stared up at it, and as the light bent and refracted on the outline of its nose and jaw, Mrs Hennypeck thought for a moment that there was something familiar about that face. The hand that had been reaching for her necklace fell back, and Mrs Hennypeck saw the figure turn and sweep away, disappearing into the night.

At once, the billows of shadow fell back, releasing their grip on the magicians.

Mr Ivy and Flintwitch were breathless, slick with fear. They clutched at their hearts and caught their breath, while Mrs Hennypeck, needing no recovery time, encouraged the magpie towards her.

It circled down, calling out, and landed on a counter a short distance away. In its beak was a black envelope. The magpie stared at Mrs Hennypeck, then dropped the envelope and took off, soaring up through Filigree's and away.

"Is everyone alright?" asked Mr Ivy.

"I thought we were done for," said Flintwitch. "Why did it let us go?"

Mrs Hennypeck picked up the magpie's envelope. "It's for you." She handed the card to Mr Ivy, who examined it, opened it and proceeded to read the message inside:

Dear Mr Ivy,

I am both sorry and curious to hear of the most terrible and unusual troubles that have befallen you. I have arrived in London, and invite you to the Nowhere Emporium in Carnaby Street in the hope that my vast knowledge and unrivalled skills might assist you in this time of need.

Kind regards,
Lucien Silver

Mr Ivy stared at the message.

"How does he manage," said Mrs Hennypeck, "to sound so smug in a letter? Unrivalled skills indeed!"

"Hold on," said Flintwitch. "That creature… Shade Walker… it had us beat, right? If it was after you, Mrs Hennypeck, why did it stop?"

"Because Lucien Silver has just arrived in London," said Mr Ivy, "and his Emporium is—"

"Filled with enough raw magic to make this Shade Walker unstoppable," finished Mrs Hennypeck. "Silver has no idea what's coming for him."

CHAPTER 29

HENNYPECK HOUSE

London, Present Day

The black Range Rover screeched around the corner, tearing past grand houses. In the driver's seat, Mr Flintwitch's eyes were fixed firmly on the road, his hands gripping the steering wheel tight. In the back, Daniel and Ellie were fastened securely. The car moved with such speed that the world seemed to blur past the windows.

"How fast are we going?" Daniel swallowed hard as Mr Flintwitch swung the huge car around another sharp bend, barrelling through a red light. "Won't the police stop us?"

At that moment a black cab came out of a side

street, pulling right into their path. Mr Flintwitch was driving far too quickly to slow down in time. They were going to collide, to smash right into each other...

Mr Flintwitch didn't even blink.

He pressed a button on the dashboard. Daniel felt something like a wave of electricity pass through his body, and when he looked down, he cried out in shock.

The car had disappeared.

Not only that, but Daniel had disappeared too; his body was still there, he could feel his arms, his legs, his face, could feel the car vibrating beneath him, but it was all invisible. He could see no Mr Flintwitch, no Ellie, only the street, like he was just a pair of eyeballs floating in mid-air.

They passed through the London cab as if they were ghosts. Flintwitch plunged the Range Rover down a side street and screeched to a halt in a fine, tree-lined avenue. He pressed the button on the dashboard again, and everything suddenly went back to being visible and solid.

Mr Flintwitch jumped out of the car and sprinted towards the tall iron gates of a grand house – a mansion. When Daniel and Ellie caught up, he was running his finger down the metal then tasting his fingertip.

Ellie brought out her hazel wand again and set it

in motion. It spun around and pointed at the house beyond the gates. Mr Flintwitch gave a nod and reached out his hand. The gates clicked and swung open.

They walked cautiously up the driveway. The mansion was made of blond stone, with tall windows and narrow, reaching chimneys. The front lawn was overgrown, and ivy had crept over a large portion of the house, coating it in twisting vines.

No lights were visible from the front of the house. The front door was slightly ajar.

Mr Flintwitch put his finger to his lips and reached for the handle, pushing the door open. Daniel's chest felt tight as he followed.

The entrance hall was cavernous and dim. A tall window by the staircase let in an eerie orange glow from the street, and everything was smothered in thick dust. It was the sort of place, Daniel thought, which used to be grand. He could imagine the hallway lavishly decorated and filled with glamorous people.

Thud.

The sound made them freeze.

"It came from somewhere at the back of the house," whispered Ellie.

"If Edna's here," Daniel told Mr Flintwitch, "don't hurt her."

Behind the staircase there was a long hallway, and at the end of the hallway an open door. From the room beyond came a girl's voice. There was a strange quality to it, as if she was asleep, crying out in the midst of a nightmare.

Daniel raised his hazel wand, his body crawling with tension and fear.

They inched inside.

The room was a kitchen. Orange city light tumbled in through a skylight, illuminating dust motes and the girl who stood in the centre of the room.

"Edna!"

"Daniel? No! Stay back!" Edna spun to face him, and her face was her own again, her eyes alive and shining and present, but filled with tears. On the floor by her feet was an abandoned shadow, like the one they'd discovered in the old man's house.

"Mrs Hennypeck!"

Mr Flintwitch ran forward and crouched over the shadow of his old colleague, but he was too late. She was gone. Tracing the edge of the shadow, he saw that before she finally left this world, she had scratched something onto the floor. Two initials.

BN

"Where's the necklace?" Flintwitch asked, pointing at Edna. "You took it!"

"No," said Edna. "I swear! I tried to stop him, but he was too strong."

Mr Flintwitch moved towards her. "Who? Tell me, girl!"

In the corner of the room, a creature detached from the shadows, a patch of darkness. It was the shape of a man, and it walked to the space between Edna and the others, the darkness that contained it swirling, becoming solid, until a real man stood before them, flesh and blood. Tall and thin, he was dressed in an old-fashioned suit and overcoat, like the ones Daniel had seen in the 1960s, and he wore a smart top hat. Around his neck, tucked beneath his clothes, was a shining necklace. He seemed puzzled at first, as he held up his hands and stared at them as if they were strange, alien things. Then he smiled, and laughed, and threw open his arms, tears of joy running down his face.

"Don't move!" came Mr Flintwitch's voice. "I'm with the Bureau!" He inched forwards, showing his badge, and the sight of it seemed to wake this strange man up. He spun around and grabbed Edna, pushing her forward like some sort of human shield.

"Edna!" Daniel shouted.

She was terrified, shaking, the whites of her eyes magnified through her huge glasses.

"I'll kill her," said the man. "You know I will." He steered her forwards slowly.

Mr Flintwitch raised his hands and indicated that Daniel and Ellie should do the same. "This is done," he said to the man. "Where are you going to go?"

The man stopped under the skylight. He looked up. Then he looked at Daniel, stared right into his eyes, and said, "I'm not done. I'm just getting started. And that shop of yours is going to help me."

He jumped straight up, through the skylight. It was a jump no everyday human could have made. As he crashed through the window, huge blades of shattered glass began to fall, almost in slow motion, towards Edna.

Daniel acted without thinking, diving forward, pushing Edna out of harm's way. He felt shards pierce his back, and the back of his legs and arms, and he began to cry out, but the pain was too much.

The world turned black.

CHAPTER 30

WELCOME TO LONDON

The Nowhere Emporium, London, 1967

Lucien Silver, proprietor of the Nowhere Emporium, sat at his desk, his battered *Book of Wonders* open before him. The scratch of his fountain pen on the page chorused with the ticking of the many clocks on the walls and the spitting song of the fire.

Those content, quiet sounds were shattered when the window of the shop exploded inwards, causing Silver to kick back in his chair in fright, crashing to the floor. Quick as he could, Silver climbed to his feet and surveyed the scene.

The window was completely blown in, and fragments of glass had spread all the way across the room, some even landing on his desk. Silver stared around in disbelief, until a faint chirping sound pulled him away from his desk and out into the shop.

He found his silver magpie on the floor and picked it up with gentle hands. It was badly damaged, moving only very slightly.

"What happened to you, my friend?" said Mr Silver. He held the bird in one hand, waved his free hand over it to repair the damage, and it was gone. Then he walked to the shattered window, the cool London night air sweeping in. Even though the hour was late and most of Carnaby Street was asleep, distant sounds of music and singing drifted on the breeze.

But there was another sound, much closer.

Footsteps, slow and deliberate.

Lucien Silver squinted out into the street. "Hello?"

There was something there; he could see it, see the edges of it catching the light. A man. Yes. He was sure of it; there was the flash of a nose, the brief glimpse of a long coat, but each time Silver thought he'd caught some new detail, it would disappear just as quick.

The figure came closer, and closer still.

Silver held up a hand. "Don't come any further. Not another step."

But the ghost, or phantom, or whatever this strange creature was, paid him no attention. It swept through the open window into the Nowhere Emporium, past Lucien Silver and towards the red velvet curtain at the back of the shop, the one leading to Mr Silver's labyrinth of Wonders.

The magician spun around, anger boiling inside him. The instinct to protect his Emporium took over, and he ran forward...

Or at least tried to run forward.

He found that he couldn't move. He stared at the phantom and pushed back against it with everything he had, every ounce of magic and power in every cell of his body.

In the space between them, there was a tearing sound, like the seams of the world were ripping, and Mr Silver fell back as a great wave of force passed through the shop. He found that he could move again, and he got up, panting, searching for some glimpse of the creature. A flash of it here. A flicker there.

Silver saw a movement on the wall and wheeled around, taking a sharp breath.

His shadow – his own shadow – cast by the warm lamps and dancing fire, was moving, changing shape, growing.

Lucien Silver had seen many things. He had travelled the world, visited places most people did not even know existed, cut through time like a sharp knife. But this... this was something new. His shadow left the wall. It billowed around him, flapping and rolling until it encircled him, cutting him off from the world, from his precious Emporium.

A familiar scene unfolded around him.

He was in a room he recognised, a grand study framed with bookcases. On the floor lay a young woman. Mr Silver recognised her at once, of course. Michelle. She had been the love of his life. He stared down at her, wiping his burning eyes, and he crouched low, placing his hand near the wound on her chest where the handle of a silver knife jutted from the flesh. Her white nightgown was stained with fresh blood.

Lucien Silver had been here before, once in reality, and countless other times in his nightmares.

"Michelle... Oh, Michelle. I'm so sorry."

Part of Lucien Silver knew that this wasn't real. He had dealt in illusion and magic for almost his entire life. But another part of him – the bigger part – was frightened and ashamed and filled with terrible sorrow. Ice seemed to encircle his heart, and all the happiness he had ever felt was drained away, leaving only despair.

And then he was falling, falling through the floor, through the vision, into darkness.

Down.

Down.

Down.

"Mr Silver!"

"Lucien!"

A sound like lightning, and suddenly he was being pulled through the dark, like a fish on a hook, up and up and up...

When Lucien Silver awakened, there were three concerned faces looking down at him. One of them was dead.

"Is that you, Mrs Hennypeck?"

Mrs Hennypeck nodded.

Silver's mind was still numb, clouded, and he was struggling to remember, to make sense of anything. He frowned. "Still, um…"

"Dead?" offered Mrs Hennypeck. "Yes I am. Well spotted."

"Are you quite all right?" asked Mr Ivy.

In that moment Lucien Silver's mind focused once more, and he scrambled up and staggered towards the curtain. "That thing… it's in my shop!"

"Hold on!" said Mr Ivy. "Look at you! You're in no condition to go after it."

Lucien Silver straightened up. He made an attempt to tidy his hair and smooth out the creases in his suit. When he spoke, his voice was low and dangerous. "Nothing threatens my Emporium. Everything that happens in here happens because *I* say so."

"If I may, sir," said young Flintwitch, "the normal rules of magic don't seem to apply to this Shade Walker. I don't doubt your ability or your power, but if you charge after this thing it'll use your own magic against you."

"And who are you?" asked Lucien Silver, looking the boy up and down.

"Flintwitch, sir."

"And what would you suggest, Flintwitch?"

The boy thought for a moment. "A trap, sir. We can't meet this thing head on, so we have to be clever about it."

"A trap," repeated Silver.

"It's after power," said Mrs Hennypeck. "It's killed several magicians, taken everything they are and left only a shadow. It was drawn to my necklace and would have taken it had you not arrived in London when you did. It sensed the magic here."

Silver held up a finger. "Power," he said. "*Power!* The Fountain!"

"The what?" asked Mr Ivy.

"It's the heart of this place. The place where the raw magic is stored."

"Then we must get there before the walker!" said Mrs Hennypeck.

Mr Silver smiled. "My dear woman, the Fountain is hidden. There's no one, indeed no *thing*, that can find it without me showing the way. And that is exactly what I'm going to do."

A pause.

"You're going to *show* it the magic?" said young Flintwitch.

Lucien Silver went to his desk and opened his

Book of Wonders. "You're welcome to help me if you like."

And as he began to write in the book, he told them his plan.

CHAPTER 31

WAITING

London, Present Day

A rectangle of light hung above Daniel, but something was blocking it. He opened his eyes wider, tried to focus, and at last recognised the shape blocking the light: Mr Flintwitch was crouching over him.

It all came rushing back – Edna and the Shade Walker and Ellie... He tried to sit up, but Mr Flintwitch held him down with a firm hand. "Don't move. The healing's almost done."

Mr Flintwitch's free hand hovered over Daniel's legs and Daniel felt warmth spreading through his body, felt the cuts and wounds closing. "Edna. Where's Edna? She OK?"

Mr Flintwitch did not answer at first. He raised a finger to his lips and continued to treat Daniel's wounds. "They aren't too deep," he said. "You were lucky…" he managed a fleeting smile, "and quite brave. There. Done."

He helped Daniel up, and Daniel saw that his shirt was open and there were streaks of blood on his chest, but no marks at all on his flesh.

"The worst of it was on your back," Mr Flintwitch told him. "But you rolled over when you passed out and a few shards hit you in the chest. There's one scar near your shoulder blade, but scars are cool, right?"

Daniel fastened his shirt. "Thanks. Where's Ellie?" He stared at the spot on the floor where Edna had been lying. "And Edna?"

Mr Flintwitch motioned for Daniel to follow and showed him to a door down the hall. It opened into a large, cold sitting room at the front of the house. There were fine sofas and paintings on the wall, and an odd smell of decay hung in the air.

Ellie sat on one of the sofas and beside her was Edna. Both of them sipped at mugs of hot tea.

"Daniel!" Ellie got up, hugged him tight.

"I'm fine," he said. "You OK?"

Ellie nodded, then Daniel turned to Edna. She looked sheepish, and there were tears in her eyes.

"Oh, I'm sorry." She stood up, wringing her hands. "I'm so, so sorry! All of this is my fault. I was in your

shop, you see, and one of the tents called out to me…"
She choked on the words. "… And my grandpa was
there! It seemed so real. But it wasn't. It wasn't real.
There was something in that tent, something that got
inside my shadow and made me do things…" She began
to sob, and Ellie and Daniel put their arms around her.

"It isn't your fault," said Daniel. "None of it, you
hear?"

"I fought him," said Edna. "I really tried at first. But
he convinced me that nobody would believe me. Told
me they'd lock me up. And the more people he hurt,
the stronger he got."

It occurred to Daniel that Mr Flintwitch hadn't
followed him in, so he left Ellie with Edna and went
back out to the hall. Again he caught glimpses of the
house's former splendour: huge mirrors with faded
ornamental frames, candelabras dressed in cobwebs.

From the kitchen came a soft, murmuring sound.
As he crept towards it, Daniel began to feel that he
was eavesdropping on a private moment, and he
thought about turning back, but a voice called to him:
"Daniel? Is that you?"

He pushed the door fully open, entered the kitchen.

Mr Flintwitch was crouching over the shadow on
the floor – all that remained of the lady of the house.

"Is that—"

"Mrs Hennypeck," said Mr Flintwitch. "Yes." He
touched the place where her face would have been.

"She was quite extraordinary, you know. Even death didn't stop her. At least not the first time."

"I'm not following."

Mr Flintwitch pointed to the shadow. "Mrs Hennypeck was dead long before tonight. She passed away many years ago."

"But I don't understand," said Daniel. "If she died so long ago, how come we rushed here tonight to try and save her? And how did this shadow appear?"

Mr Flintwitch pointed to the shadow's neck. "She wore a necklace. The story I always heard was that Mrs Hennypeck was a woman of very considerable means. She knew she was going to die – an illness of some sort that neither magic nor medicine could cure – and so she set about finding an object that would allow her to stick around after death."

Daniel took a sharp breath. "Like a zombie?"

"What? No! She had a blueish tinge, but nothing like a zombie. When she died, the necklace allowed her soul to remain tethered to her body, just as in life, and it enabled her to move and think; as long as she wore the necklace, it would stay that way."

"I suppose that explains all the dust then – it couldn't make her sneeze if she didn't need to breathe." Daniel tried to imagine what it might have been like to see a little old dead woman walking and talking. "Hey! The guy we saw in the kitchen was wearing something shiny under his shirt!"

Mr Flintwitch nodded. "He killed her for the necklace. The power of it will magnify his strength."

Suddenly there was a great pressing on Daniel's chest. A darkness seemed to reach around him, squeezing him tight. He stumbled back and slid down a nearby kitchen cupboard. Every breath was a fight to force air into his lungs, his blood. Visions flashed in his mind, of the Emporium, of a stranger creeping through the Wonders, searching for something…

He managed to stand. The tightness was loosening. He could breathe again.

"He's in the Nowhere Emporium!"

Mr Flintwitch nodded.

"What is he?" asked Daniel.

"A Shade Walker, I think. A magician who's turned so bad he has become shadow and darkness. A shapeshifter who feeds on the magic of others."

"He's after the Fountain!"

"How long have you been in charge, Daniel? Six months?"

"Yeah. How did you know?"

"I've been following your career with interest since Mr Silver passed away."

"You knew Papa?" Ellie had quietly entered the kitchen.

Mr Flintwitch's brow creased. "I was very sorry to hear of your father's passing. He was a great magician."

Ellie folded her arms, seemed almost to hug herself. "Thank you. Did you know him well?"

Mr Flintwitch indicated the shadow on the floor. "I've hunted this creature once before, many years ago, when I was still a child and new to the Bureau. Mrs Hennypeck and Mr Ivy – the two magicians who died tonight – were my senior officers. The thing is, Mr Silver and the Nowhere Emporium were involved back then too."

"They were?" said Ellie. "He was?"

"Come," said Mr Flintwitch. "We must get to your shop. I'll explain on the way."

They collected Edna and jumped into Flintwitch's black Range Rover, and as he started the engine and began the drive towards the Emporium, he told them the story of a night very long ago.

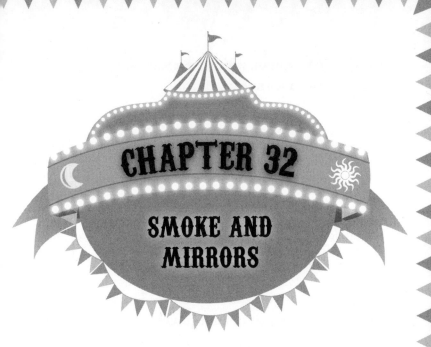

CHAPTER 32

SMOKE AND MIRRORS

The Nowhere Emporium, London, 1967

Lucien Silver led Mr Ivy and the others through his Emporium, a labyrinth of tangled black brick passageways full of secrets, like the man himself. All the while he knew that something was watching.

"This place really is astonishing," marvelled Mr Ivy. "How many rooms?"

"Wonders? I've lost count. But the one we're going to now is the most important of the lot. It powers the entire shop, and I want to make sure this Shade Walker creature hasn't damaged it in any way."

On they went, down many stairs, until they came

to a black door upon which there was a shining golden sign inscribed with two words.

Lucien Silver reached for the door handle and looked around at the others. Then he opened the door.

A cold breath of winter air escaped from the room beyond, and they stepped through the doorway into a woodland clearing. The surrounding trees were coated in a thick dusting of frost, the sky was clear and brilliant blue, and the air smelled crisp and fresh.

They were standing on the surface of a frozen pond, and in the centre of the pond was a fountain: three tiers of circular stone, over which a silvery liquid was flowing.

"That," said Mr Silver, "is imagination. Magic in its purest form. Thank heavens it's safe. Why, if anything was to happen to it…" He stopped talking and spun around, looking out towards the open doorway among the trees.

As he had expected, there was the Walker, almost invisible, the light from the sun catching the edges of it, highlighting details for brief moments – the shape of a nose, fingers, feet.

Lucien Silver ran across the frozen pond, his shoes crunching in the thick frost. He positioned himself between the creature and the fountain.

"Back!" He pointed towards the creature. But his own shadow was moving again, rising up from the ice, wrapping around him. "No. No!" He kicked, pushed, heard screams and shouts from nearby as Mr Ivy and the others struggled too. His shadow held him in place, made him watch as the creature moved to the fountain, and circled it. The sunlight gleamed on the edges of a hand, reaching out…

It touched the silver liquid.

The world dissolved around them.

The fountain vanished. So too did the woods. In the beat of a heart, all that remained of the Wonder was the ice, and the blue sky, and the sun. And mirrors. A circle of ornately framed mirrors had appeared around the perimeter of the ice. Each mirror was positioned to reflect the glaring sun towards the same spot, concentrated on the creature.

Mr Silver's shadow fell back, and he stalked slowly towards the centre of the ice, to where the Shade Walker was thrashing and screaming, unable to escape the burning beams of sunlight. Within the blazing light, the creature's true shape became clearly visible. It was a man, made of light, his features burning so brightly that nobody could look directly at them.

"Now!" cried Lucien Silver.

Simultaneously, the four magicians cast a spell, opening up one of the mirrors, turning it into a gateway. The gateway pulled at the creature, dragging it across the ice. The screams from it were almost unbearable, and Silver felt as if the walker was taking a razor to his thoughts, but he kept the spell going; everyone did, giving everything they had, every ounce of magic.

"You think I would be stupid enough to lead you to the real Fountain?" yelled Silver.

The monster was almost at the mirror now, its feet scraping on the ice, leaving deep grooves. But still the spell pulled, still the mirror dragged it inward. Half of it was through now, into whatever place lay behind the glass. The mirror shook, trembled, and for a moment Lucien Silver was fearful that it might shatter and the creature would be free. But the mirror held, until all that was left of the monstrous thing was a hand – a single hand reaching, clawing at the air. With one final, distant scream, the mirror swallowed the last of it, and the surface rippled.

The silence was deafening after all that thunderous sound. Only one ornate mirror remained, the one that mattered most – the mirror in which the Shade Walker was trapped.

Lucien Silver stood before the mirror, hands on hips, and his reflection was joined by those of Mr Ivy and Mrs Hennypeck and Flintwitch. Beyond their reflections, deep in the mirror, a shadowy form was swirling. It charged forward and banged on the glass, causing Mr Ivy to jump back.

"Don't worry," Lucien Silver told him. "It won't get out. Not unless something damages that mirror. Which won't happen; I'll lock it away deep in the Emporium."

"We should take it away," said Mr Ivy. "It's our duty to make sure it causes no more harm."

Silver leaned casually on the heavy mirror. A faint howl echoed from deep inside.

"My dear Mr Ivy, I assure you that I would like nothing more than for you to take this thing far from my shop. Unfortunately, the magic that binds it in the mirror exists only within the boundaries of the Nowhere Emporium. The moment the mirror travels through the curtain, the monster will be free. Alas, I'm afraid it's stuck here. But I give you my word, Mr Ivy, that I will keep a watchful eye over this mirror. I will lock it away from the world. The monster is gone. The people of London are safe once more."

Flintwitch let out a spirited "Hooray!" but no one else joined in, so he shrank back and fell silent.

"Then I suppose we have no choice." Mr Ivy patted Silver on the shoulder, sending a cloud of dust into the clean air. "Thank you, Lucien, for aiding us in this dark time. You are an eminently powerful magician."

Mr Silver nodded grimly. "That immense talent weighs heavily on my shoulders, I assure you. It is my duty, from time to time, to step in and help those… less proficient."

Mrs Hennypeck rolled her eyes. "And you've stayed so modest, too…"

"Let us treat you to dinner," offered Mr Ivy, interjecting before Silver could reply.

Silver scratched his stubbly chin. "I'm not much of an eater. I've always considered hunger to be something of an inconvenience."

"Then I thoroughly recommend dying," said Mrs Hennypeck. "I haven't eaten for forty years."

Mr Ivy wagged a finger thoughtfully. "You know, we have quite a collection of rare and ancient magical artefacts back at the Bureau. Strictly for the eyes of investigators, of course – but I'm sure we can make an exception this once."

"Now that," said Mr Silver, "I *am* interested in…"

They walked back to the darkened hallways of the Emporium. As the door closed on the room, the mirror trembled, and the creature behind the glass screamed into the silence.

CHAPTER 33

NO MORE HIDING

London, Present Day

Mr Flintwitch jammed on the brakes of his black Range Rover, bringing the car to a skidding halt in front of the Nowhere Emporium.

Daniel and the others piled from the car, ran through the rain and into the shop. No sooner had Daniel stepped through the door than he felt the power of the place returning to his body. He closed his eyes, concentrated on the countless Wonders and felt another heartbeat somewhere in the endless carnival.

"He's here somewhere… I just can't get a fix on him." He kicked out at a table in frustration, sending gems and glittering jewels scattering to the floor.

"Why wouldn't Papa tell you about this?" said Ellie. "Surely he should have warned you that there was a dangerous creature trapped in the Emporium when you took over!"

Daniel sighed. "He did have his hands full, you know, trying not to get killed. And the handover did happen in a bit of a rush. I suppose he never left any memory of it in the *Book of Wonders* or in his echo because he was trying to keep us safe. I mean, if we didn't know about it, we couldn't go near it, could we?"

"I don't mean to stick my nose in..." said Edna.

"Oh, I think you've earned that right," Daniel told her.

"Oh. Thanks! Well, I was going to say, what'll happen if this thing actually finds the Fountain?"

"There's no chance of that. I'm the only one who can find the Fountain. Not even Ellie..." Daniel's world juddered, and suddenly he was somewhere else, seeing through eyes that weren't his own. He was walking through the carnival, through the curtained entrance to a tent, and on the other side... a woodland clearing, blue sky, frost, ice...

And then Daniel was back in his own head.

"Impossible," he said, a knot of dread tightening in his gut.

"What? What's impossible?" asked Mr Flintwitch. "Speak to us, Daniel!"

He stared around their tired, concerned faces. "He's done it. He's found the Fountain!"

They ran.

They ran through the curtain to the Carnival of Wonders, twisting and turning between endless rows of tents and stalls under the always-twilight sky. They ran through the staff campsite, where Emporium performers stood like stone statues around the fire. With every step Daniel's panic grew, until he could barely breathe.

"Here," he said, panting. "This way."

They had come to a woodland area among the tents, a patch of redwood trees that almost scratched the sky. Scattered high among the branches were treehouses spilling warm golden light.

"Up there?" asked Ellie.

"Nope. This way." Daniel led them between the trunks of the gigantic trees, until he stopped at one and reached out a hand. To the great surprise of the others, Daniel pulled open a hidden door in the trunk. The scent of winter breathed from the opening, of frost and clean air, and Daniel hurried through, his feet crunching down on the icy surface beyond.

He looked around the frozen pond, the surrounding frost-covered forest and the stone fountain in the centre of it all. Pure, silvery magic was flowing serenely over the three tiers of stone. All was well.

"He's not here," said Daniel, as Ellie and the others joined him on the ice.

"Maybe he went somewhere else?" suggested Edna, trying to shake some warmth back into her fingers.

"No," said Daniel, "I saw him. He was here, and he was going after the Fountain, after the imagination…"

"He's quite right, you know."

The voice did not belong to Daniel, or Ellie, or Edna, or Mr Flintwitch. They spun around, turned to the doorway where he stood, tall and thin, dressed in old-fashioned clothes. He took a few steps forward onto the ice.

Crunch.

Crunch.

Crunch.

Mr Flintwitch drew his hazel, and Ellie followed suit, but the man merely curled his lip and the hazel flew out of their hands, spinning away across the pond.

"As I was saying, Mr Holmes is correct. He did see me here – but only because I put the vision in his head. I couldn't find the Fountain, you see. I knew it was here, but it was too well hidden. So I needed you to show me. And what better way of doing that than by having you race here and open the door for me?"

"What do we do, Daniel?" asked Ellie.

"There's nothing you can do, dear," said the man.

"I've waited too long to be denied." He took another few steps towards the Fountain. "Do you know how long I spent trapped in this place? Locked up on the other side of that mirror? And before that, trapped in limbo? In the space between worlds?"

"You have killed," said Mr Flintwitch, "and tortured. And among your victims were friends of mine—"

"Friends? Let me tell you about *friends*, Mr Flintwitch. I thought I had friends once. I was a member of your Bureau. I was sent to fight a monster with my so-called friends. A Shade Walker. And do you know what happened when that Shade Walker turned me into a phantom? A ghost? Do you know what happened then, Mr Flintwitch? My Bureau *friends* forgot about me. They told my family I was dead! I spent years watching my loved ones grow old and die. My friends forgot about me, so I punished them. I cast them into the dark and took their power so that I might be whole again."

Mr Flintwitch stepped forward. "The Bureau sent you to fight a Shade Walker?" His eyes searched, his mind working to put the pieces together.

"That's it," said the man. "You'll get there. You have all the information…"

"What's 'it', Mr Flintwitch?" asked Daniel. "What's he talking about?"

"The Needle Incident." Mr Flintwitch's voice was barely more than a whisper.

The man clapped his hands. "I knew you'd get there in the end!"

"You?" said Mr Flintwitch. "*You're* Bob Needle? You're the one who vanished on the night Mrs Hennypeck went to fight the Shade Walker? All this time… all these years we thought we were looking for the Shade Walker who killed you, when we should have been looking for you." He hung his head. "I'm sorry for what happened to you. But you've caused so much pain. You must pay for that."

"If you stand in my way, I'll make sure you join those friends of yours." Bob Needle moved towards the Fountain. As he did so, Daniel reached for the *Book of Wonders*, but Needle lazily waved a finger and the book spun off into the woodland. Daniel's shadow rose up from the ice, along with the shadows of his friends, billowing and surrounding them, holding them in place, making them watch as Needle reached the Fountain.

Daniel fought with everything he had. Slick with sweat from the effort, he pushed back against the shadow. But he couldn't budge it. Then, as Needle reached out towards the Fountain, Daniel seemed to wake up.

This is my Emporium. My world! He might be stronger than me, but Mr Silver's magic still runs through the walls, and I can control it!

He closed his eyes, and thought of the ice under

Needle's feet, imagined it melting. Needle froze as the sound of cracking ice filled the woodland clearing. He looked down to see the surface fracturing beneath him. He started to run, but the ice gave way and he fell through into the freezing water beneath.

Immediately Needle's spell was broken. The shadows that had been holding Daniel and the others retreated. Where Needle had fallen through, Daniel's imagination was creating new ice, layer upon layer, locking Needle beneath the surface.

He spun to face the others. "Go!"

As they ran for the door, the ground began to tremble, gently at first, but gathering strength, until it became difficult to stay standing and it seemed the trees were shaking so madly they would topple over.

A hand burst through the ice.

Needle clawed himself out of the pond and stood, sodden, beside the Fountain. He cupped his hands together, dipped them into the flowing silver magic and lifted them to his mouth. He shot Daniel a smile.

Then he drank.

CHAPTER 34

FIGHT AND FLIGHT

The Nowhere Emporium, London, Present Day

"Run! Get out!" Daniel's mind was spinning, bursting with horror and fear as he guided his friends out of the Fountain, through the door to the Carnival of Wonders.

"What's going to happen?" asked Edna as they darted through the redwood trees. "Why's it so bad that he drank from the Fountain?"

"Because he drank imagination – pure magic! One sip would drive any normal person mad, rip their mind to shreds…"

Cold laughter came booming from behind, and Daniel and his friends took cover behind a tent.

Footsteps.

Needle's voice echoed all around them, filling every part of the carnival, filling Daniel's mind.

"For so long I was adrift," he said. "Suffering. Weak. But look at me now. You're done, Daniel Holmes, you and your friends. There's no way to beat me now."

When they glanced around the corner of the tent, they saw him some distance away. His eyes glowed dazzling silver, like the magic from the Fountain, and sparks jumped between his fingertips.

"Mr Flintwitch! No!"

Mr Flintwitch had stepped out into the open and stood facing Needle. "Bob Needle! I'm arresting you for the murder of seven magicians. You will come with me to Bureau Headquarters, where you will await trial. If you do not come quietly, I will take you by force."

Bob Needle laughed. A tangle of huge roots erupted from the ground beneath Mr Flintwitch's feet. The roots surrounded him, twining and coiling into the shape of a cage, trapping him inside. Mr Flintwitch tried to use his hazel, but the cage would not break.

Daniel turned to his friends. He could hardly believe what he was about to say.

"You have to get out of the shop. Not just out of the carnival, but the whole place. Out into the street."

Ellie looked into his eyes. "What are you going to do, Daniel?"

"I'm going to stop Needle from ever getting back out into the world."

"I know you're here, Daniel," said Needle's booming voice. "I can smell you. No grown-ups to protect you now!"

A large explosion ripped the air, and a nearby tent exploded, sending smoke and flames high into the twilight.

"Why Daniel?" Ellie demanded. "I have a right to know what you're going to do with this place. It's my home."

Daniel knew that she wouldn't leave him, not without being pushed. He didn't want to hurt her, but he had to keep her safe, keep all of them safe…

"Get out!" he screamed. "This isn't your home any more, is it? You said so yourself – you want things to change, want to live your life. So go! Do it! I don't need you!"

"Daniel," Ellie's eyes were welling up, "what are you doing?"

"Your dad is gone," said Daniel coldly. "The shop belongs to me now, and it's up to me to deal with this. If Needle goes back out into the world he'll be unstoppable. How many people will die? But in here, in the Emporium, I have a chance. I'm going to find the *Book of Wonders*, and I'm going to destroy it.

When that happens, this place, and everything in it, will be gone – including Needle. You don't want to be here when that happens."

Ellie shook her head. She stared at him like he had turned into something strange and horrifying.

Daniel stepped back and closed his eyes. A wall erupted from the ground, stretching as far as he could see, cutting him off from his friends. On the other side he heard Ellie scream, and yell, and curse, and the sound of her suffering made him feel sick. But he turned around and stepped out into the open.

"I can't let you leave," he said.

Needle stood across the grass. "I don't believe I gave you a choice."

Daniel made a move. Thorny vines burst from the ground at Needle's feet, wrapped around him, twining and squeezing, and for the briefest moment Daniel had hope that it might work, that Needle would be trapped for long enough to let him get the book.

But the vines turned black and withered, and dropped to the ground in limp piles.

Needle flicked a finger, and his shadow rose up from the earth, grew so huge that it seemed to fill the entire sky, a gigantic patch of darkness billowing in the breeze as if it was made of fine silk.

Needle swiped a hand, and as he did so his shadow mimicked his movement; a giant hand made of darkness came crashing down. Daniel was quick enough to dive out of the way as the hand tore past, carving a deep channel in the ground, ripping apart huge tents like they were toys. When Needle stamped a foot, the shadow's foot came down with such force that the world of the Emporium shook, sending Daniel tumbling, and he could do nothing as the shadow reached down and wrapped around him. Needle's shadow lifted him up, held him so high he could see the tents of his beloved carnival stretching for miles.

"It'll be over soon." Needle's voice seemed to be inside Daniel's head now. "One more meal for the road, I think."

The shadow squeezed Daniel, and he felt fear pierce his heart.

Needle's shadow had crashed through the wall like it was made of matchsticks. Now, among the tangled wreckage of the tents beyond, Ellie Silver opened her eyes and saw a face peering down at her, a face made entirely of cogs and gears that had arranged themselves into an expression of deep concern.

"Ringmaster?"

"Miss Ellie! Thank goodness you're alright!"

The clockwork ringmaster helped Ellie up. Her body ached almost as much as her heart did.

"Have you seen the others? Edna and Mr Flintwitch? They were with me when…"

A groan nearby, and a pile of debris shifted and up came Edna, covered in dust and dirt. There was blood in the corner of her mouth and one of the lenses of her glasses was completely shattered.

Ellie limped towards her. "You all right?"

"I think so. Where's Mr Flintwitch?"

"I'm here." Flintwitch emerged from the smoke, now free of his cage. His fine black suit was torn and his face was smeared with blood. "Now I'm angry."

"Look," said Edna. "It's got Daniel!"

Ellie turned to see the huge shadow filling the sky. She stared up and spotted Daniel in its grip. "Mr Flintwitch," she said, "please make sure Edna gets home safely."

Flintwitch and Edna shared a knowing look.

"Oh no you don't!" Edna told her. "You don't get to march out there like this is some old cowboy movie and face him down alone. He's hurt all of us, and we all want him to pay. I'm coming with you."

Mr Flintwitch gave a small bow. "Bureau of Magical Investigation at your service, ma'am."

Ellie's heart was filled with such gratitude that she felt lighter, stronger, felt ready to face whatever was about to happen, because she would not face it alone.

"Come on," she said. "Let's give Daniel a fighting chance."

CHAPTER 35

ELLIE'S SPARK

The Nowhere Emporium, Present Day

High above, in the grasp of Needle's shadow, Daniel screamed out in terror. Every fear, every terrible thing that had ever happened to him, was surrounding him, sucking the energy from him, slowly turning him into nothing but shadow.

And then, suddenly, the grip loosened a little.

Somewhere in the blur of pain he heard Needle's voice.

"Ah! You've come out to play!"

Daniel cracked open his eyes and stared down towards the faraway ground. He saw his friends approaching Needle, trying to help, risking their lives for him, for the Nowhere Emporium. The thought of them, and the realisation that he was not alone, pushed the cold fingers out of his heart, gave him strength enough to fight back against the darkness. He pushed harder, and harder still, until at last he broke free.

He fell.

Down on the ground, the Emporium staff – all of the vendors and performers Needle had turned to stone – had begun to move. Still under Needle's spell, they surrounded Ellie and the others, and they closed in. Edna and Mr Flintwitch were casting spells, sending the statues tumbling back. But there were so many of them…

A cold stone hand grabbed Ellie's arm, spun her around, and she looked up into Caleb the Fire Breather's face. It was blank, emotionless. He reared back, brought down a fist the size of a bowling ball…

The Ringmaster blocked the blow, his metal arm buckling, and sent Caleb crashing back into the other statues.

In the centre of it all, Needle let out a scream of frustration, and Ellie's head snapped up, her eyes finding Daniel. He had fought his way free, but now he was falling, falling…

Later, when she looked back on what happened

next, Ellie could not quite explain it. It was as if the connection with the Emporium she'd always longed for, the connection her father was so disappointed never to see, was suddenly made. She felt the place in her blood, her veins, the power of it wrapping around her.

She closed her eyes, and imagined...

Daniel landed on something soft, something that was moving at tremendous speed through the air. A magic carpet! Hardly able to believe it, wondering where it had come from, he sat up as it spun and twisted high above the peaks of even the tallest carnival tents.

"Take me to the Fountain!" he yelled.

"No!" Needle's voice rumbled through the carnival. He swiped and swatted at the magic carpet, but it was so nimble, so quick, that it avoided every blow of the giant shadow with graceful ease. Down the carpet dived, towards the redwood trees.

Almost there.

And then another idea flashed bright in Daniel's mind. "No!" he said. "Not the Fountain! The Exit instead!"

The carpet pulled up, soaring high, dodging another swipe from the shadow's hands. It blazed across the sky like a shooting star. The entire way, billows of shadow were chasing, trying to wrap around the carpet, to bring it down, but somehow each time it avoided them. And then they were diving, and Daniel could see the Exit archway, see the red curtain.

He stood up on the carpet.

The shadows closed in.

The carpet swooped low over the ground.

Daniel jumped.

He hit the ground rolling, bounced through the red curtain and crashed into a table in the shopfront, sending books, papers and tin soldiers flying. His mind whirred with hope and possibility as he leapt up and dashed to the instrument on the wall with many dials and hands.

Daniel adjusted the dials, then went to the fire and picked up a handful of coal from the bucket.

He took a deep breath.

He tossed the coal into the fire.

The world lurched.

The fire roared.

The flames became so bright it seemed they'd burn through the walls between worlds, and then they faded and became red, exploding in a plume of soot. Daniel rushed to the door, opened it, and looked out.

The Nowhere Emporium was no longer in London.

He heard the sound of water, saw the branches of trees all around.

And then he heard a voice.

"Here. Who's that?"

Ellie, Mr Flintwitch, Edna and the Ringmaster were packed in a tight group, pinned together by the surrounding enchanted Emporium performers. Stone hands grasped at them, clawed and scratched.

The world – *the entire world* – lurched.

The stone hands stopped grasping. The staff became still, lifeless.

The giant black tangle of Bob Needle's shadow filling the sky swirled and shrunk and snapped back towards its owner.

Through the chaos of statues, Ellie watched as Needle sniffed at the air. His face contorted into a muddled mixture of confusion and curiosity. The silver glow in his eyes blazed, and in a swirl of smoke, he was gone. Everything was suddenly still.

Edna sent a few of the surrounding statues scattering like bowling pins, creating a way through to freedom. "Where did he go?"

"Towards the exit," said Ellie. "Daniel didn't go to the Fountain. He's not trying to destroy the Emporium after all. He's planning something else."

Mr Flintwitch gave Ellie a knowing look. "Then we go too," he said. "We help him."

"Together?" said Ellie.

Edna nodded. "Together."

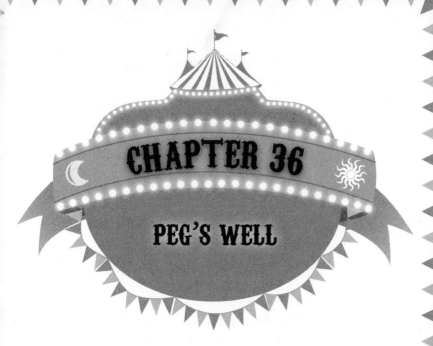

CHAPTER 36

PEG'S WELL

Keswick, Present Day

Daniel careered through the woodland, striking tree trunks and tripping over low branches until at last he broke through into clean air. He stumbled and landed hard on a stony surface. Picking himself up, he was greatly relieved to realise that he was exactly where he had aimed to be – on a familiar stony little beach, with the waves of a great lake lapping gently under the bright moon.

There was a woman standing shin-deep in the water, barefoot, staring up at the sky. When she heard the commotion, she turned around. As her eyes rested on Daniel, Peg's face became an almost comical mixture of confusion, amazement and annoyance.

"What you doin' back? You've only just left!"

Daniel got up. "What? No I haven't!"

"No?" Peg dragged him by the arm further onto the beach and pointed up to the dark sky at something small flying among the stars. "Then who's that?"

Daniel stared. "That's… that's us? Ellie and me? On the magic carpet on the way to Edinburgh?"

Peg nodded and looked up to her left. "I know," she said to someone Daniel couldn't see. "He's sharp as a tack." Then, to Daniel, "I take it, since you're back here, that things didn't go well?"

Daniel ran a hand through his hair. "I'm sorry, Peg. I didn't know where else to go. I brought him here. He's too powerful…"

From among the trees came an enormous crash, and the night filled with a harsh wind and a screeching roar. Out from the woodland strode Bob Needle. The silvery glow of his eyes was dazzling in the dark. Sparks of pure magic crackled at his fingertips.

"Oh my," muttered Peg. "What are you, now? You're all wrong. All twisted up inside."

Needle sniffed at the air. "So much magic here," he said to himself, and he turned and tilted his head towards Peg. His shadow billowed up again, reached into the sky and blocked out the stars.

Peg stared up, her mouth hanging open. "Well, he's

a big 'un, isn't he?" She spun towards Daniel. "You still got your hazel?"

"No. I lost it."

"Don't matter. Just stay close. Take my hand."

He did as she asked. Her old hands were rough and cold and bony. She raised her own hazel, and then she began to slowly move it around in the air, like a conductor. When she spoke, it was a language Daniel did not recognise, a series of strange, musical sounds, and the hum of it drifted up through the night. Whatever those words were, Bob Needle did not like them; he screeched and screamed, and his giant shadow lashed out with dark arms. Daniel could suddenly feel a great weight pressing down upon him, driving his feet into the sand.

"He's strong!" Peg said, breaking off from her chanting for a moment. "Don't let him frighten you! Don't give in, Daniel!"

Her grip tightened on his hand. She held her wand firm and pointed it skyward. Daniel saw that it was bending, like something was pressing on it. It curved dangerously, like a fishing rod with a great fish on the line, bending so far that he was sure it would snap. At the same time, the dark force pushed on him, made his spine bend, his muscles seize and cramp.

He dropped to his knees, stared up, wide-eyed, full of fear, at this strange creature, this half-man, half-monster from another world. Beside him, Peg fell too, and even though she was now on her knees she continued to chant and fight, but her voice was growing weak, getting lost in the rushing moan of a great gale that was thundering around her island. Branches were breaking from the trees, flying up into the air, far across the lake, and the waves were growing, the surface of the lake becoming choppy and capped with churning foam.

Daniel could not fight any more. He sunk down, began to curl up, the fear pressing down on him with so much force he felt he would surely be crushed.

A warm hand grabbed his wrist.

Ellie was standing over him, her eyes burning with fury and determination. She helped him up, and the touch of her hand gave him strength. He felt the fear loosen its grip. Beside him, Peg was getting up too, helped by Edna and Mr Flintwitch.

They linked arms, the five magicians, warmth and strength passing between them. Peg's chanting voice became so powerful that they could hear it over the gale, over the shrieks of the great shadow, and the sound of it vibrated in Daniel's chest.

He knew he was with friends, and that he could face anything with them at his side.

A coil of black snaked through the air towards them, a thread hanging from the shadow, twisting and winding through the night. Closer and closer it came, until it was only feet away, and then inches, until it touched the tip of Peg's hazel twig.

Peg let out an echoing, guttural yell. A shockwave erupted through her, burst out from the tip of the wand, and in the sky the great shadow let out a terrible scream and exploded, scattering out across the sky in a million fragments of midnight. The pieces turned to dust, and went with the wind.

Needle dropped to his knees, and the necklace beneath his clothes, the one that had belonged to Mrs Hennypeck, shattered. Now Needle was fading, becoming that translucent creature once more, the moonlight bending as it passed through him.

Peg flicked her wand, and the glassy, almost-invisible man separated into two parts. One was a dark coil of twisted shadow – the Shade Walker. The other was a ghostly image of Bob Needle. He floated above the ground, stared at Peg, at Daniel and the others, and they could see that the wild look, the anger and bitterness, were gone from his face.

"Go," said Peg. "Go now. You're free."

The ghost of Needle smiled and nodded. "Thank you." Then it disintegrated into sparkling dust, scattered to the wind, leaving only the dark coil twisting in the air.

Peg walked through the woodland towards her cottage, Daniel and the others following, her wand pointed at the creature, dragging it after her. She stopped beside the old well, then flicked her wand. The coil of shadow began to spin like water circling a plughole, until eventually it disappeared down the well into endless darkness.

Daniel looked at Ellie, smiled at Edna and Mr Flintwitch. They began to laugh, to holler and whoop and dance around among the overgrown trees.

CHAPTER 37

NEW BEGINNINGS

The Nowhere Emporium, Keswick, Present Day

"How's that? Better?"

Daniel scribbled another line in the *Book of Wonders*, and as the ink hit the page, a series of clicks and pings came from the Ringmaster's body and he flexed his mechanical arms.

"Better," he said, the cogs and wheels of his face arranging into a smile. "Thank you kindly, Master Daniel."

They were in the great Carnival of Wonders once more; much of it was ruined, the tents torn down and ripped apart. As soon as Needle had been defeated, his dark enchantments had lifted, and the Emporium staff, the performers and vendors, had become flesh and blood again. Now they were combing through the debris, the ragged remains of Wonders, to see what might be salvaged.

"It's going to take ages to put this right." Daniel aimed a kick at a juggling ball. "So many rooms need to be rewritten. Look at this!" He opened the book and fanned through the pages, showing the iron Ringmaster a great many passages that had been smudged. There were even pages where some of the letters and words had fallen off completely. Daniel scratched his head.

"At least, Master Daniel, there is still an Emporium to fix."

Daniel looked up from the book. "You're right. Everyone's OK, and that's what matters. All this…" he motioned to the carnival wasteland, "…all this can be fixed. It's not like I have anything else to do."

Caleb the fire breather came past then, carrying a thick wooden post over his shoulder. When he saw Daniel and the Ringmaster, he put the post down (almost crushing Daniel's feet) and approached, his hands outstretched.

"Once again, Daniel, I am so sorry for what I did. For what we all did!"

Daniel rolled his eyes. "Relax, Caleb. I already told you, it's fine."

"Fine?" said Caleb. "Fine! We tried to kill you!

I ruined the Ringmaster's arm! The shame of it all might destroy me!"

"You were under the spell of a crazed dark magician, and you had turned to stone. I think, under the circumstances, we can forgive you."

Caleb grabbed the Ringmaster's newly repaired hand and shook it vigorously.

"Oi!" said Daniel. "I've just fixed that. Let's try to keep him in one piece, shall we? Hey, can you two hold the fort here? There's somewhere I need to be."

When he walked out of the Nowhere Emporium, Daniel took a deep breath of Keswick's cold winter air. The sky was blue and clear, and the morning frost had not yet melted. The Emporium was nestled among thick, tangled trees; it looked like a strange relic from a forgotten civilisation.

As he approached Peg's cottage, Daniel heard the sound of laughter, and when he opened the door, warmth spilled out and the smell of frying bacon wrapped around him. He rubbed his empty belly.

"There he is!" Peg turned from her place at the stove, where she had three different frying pans on the go. "Just in time for breakfast! You got that Emporium of yours fixed yet?"

"Nearly," said Daniel. "I think we're just about ready to go. After breakfast of course."

They sat at the wooden table, the five friends. Peg piled bacon and eggs and sausages and black pudding high on plates in the centre of the table, and they all dug in. Daniel could not remember the last time he enjoyed a meal so much.

"So, what's the plan?" Peg asked him. "Where to next, eh?" She looked to the corner of the room and glowered at her invisible friend. "Don't you be rude!"

"Oh, I don't know," said Daniel. "Somewhere nice and quiet. I could do with a few weeks of mind-numbing boredom after this. What d'you reckon, Ellie?"

She smiled and laughed, but Daniel noticed that she couldn't quite meet his eye.

He turned back to Peg. "How about you?"

"Oh, she's going to be very busy!" said Edna through a mouthful of bacon. "Peg will be teaching me. I'm going to help her around here from now on!"

Daniel raised an eyebrow. "She is? You *are*? I thought you hated visitors."

"She won't be a visitor," Peg said. "She'll be workin' hard, or else she'll be on the first boat back to the mainland."

"Oh, I'll work hard alright." Edna bobbed up and down in her chair with excitement. One of the lenses in her glasses had been smashed, so one eye looked completely normal, while the other was still hugely magnified. "You might find this hard to believe, but I've always been a bit of an outcast. And I never believed in myself. I never thought I'd be capable of anything but taking over from Mum, and that I'd live out my days selling potion ingredients. I never imagined I'd ever leave Keswick. Ha! And look what's happened! If I can go through so much and still come out the other side in one piece, than I can do anything. And this is what I want to do. I want to keep people safe."

"I think you're very brave," said Ellie. "And you have friends in this room, Edna. Friends forever."

Edna smiled around the table, almost glowing with happiness. Then her face fell. "The hardest thing of all will be telling Mum I'm going into the monster-wrangling business. She can be scarier than any creature from another world!"

Everyone laughed.

They finished breakfast, and Daniel helped Peg wash up the dishes.

"Why don't you use magic for this?" he asked.

Peg was turning the plates and cutlery and glasses around in the water and passing them to Daniel, who dried them and stacked them away.

"Sometimes, Daniel, it's good to get back to basics. Magic is good, but too much of it can be a bad thing. If you surround yourself with nothing but magic, you'll lose touch with the real world, with people. You must learn from the mistakes of those who came before you."

Daniel looked right into her eyes, and he understood. "I used to want to be just like Mr Silver. And I still think he was a good man. But from now on I'm going to do things my way. And I'll be sure to keep in touch with the real world."

Peg reached up and tapped him on the temple. "Good lad."

After breakfast, Daniel walked through the woodland to the little strip of pebbly beach for one last look around. He sat down on a log and watched the water, breathing in the bracing winter air, and thought about everything that had happened.

After a while, he heard someone brushing through the woods. Ellie appeared from the trees, and sat next to him on the log. For a while they said nothing, just sat in silence as the sunlight shattered among the branches and fell upon the beach in golden fragments.

At last, without looking at her, Daniel spoke. "You're leaving, aren't you?"

A hesitation.

"Mr Flintwitch has offered me a job at the Bureau. He says there's untapped potential in me and that I could be a great Magical Investigator. Me! Good at something!"

"He must be barking," said Daniel jokingly before

turning to look at her with great seriousness. "I think you should take the job."

Ellie looked surprised. "You do?"

"Yeah. I mean… I don't *want* you to go, Ellie. I really don't. You're the best friend I ever had. But that's why I know you *need* to go. I've been selfish. All this time, I've only been thinking about how taking over the Emporium has changed *my* life. I expected everything to stay the same, to revolve around me, and I know that's not how it works. I never thought about how it must feel for you, living in the same place you spent your whole life in with your dad. It must feel like you're trapped, like you can't move on. I'm sorry."

Ellie brushed the curls from her face, and he saw that there were tears in her eyes, catching the sunlight.

"Will you come visit me?" she asked.

"Are you kidding? Just try and stop me."

"Promise?"

"Yeah. Promise."

They sat in silence again, comfortable silence, and watched the ferry from Keswick drift by in the distance.

"You're going to be great, you know," she said at last. "Better than great. Brilliant. Papa always thought so. He might have been a bit of a loony, but he got that right."

"You take care now," Peg told Daniel, pulling him in for a tight hug.

"You too. And Peg… you should know… your brother – he misses you. He worries about you."

Peg's old eyes became a little wet at the edges. "You best be on your way. And Daniel?"

"Yes?"

"Try not to come back any time soon."

He laughed. "I'll try, Peg."

Edna was next. She wrapped her arms around him and squeezed him tight. "Thank you," she said. "I'm so glad you came to Keswick. I always knew the Emporium would be wonderful, but I didn't expect the best thing of all to be the people inside it."

"Take care, Edna."

Daniel turned to Mr Flintwitch. "Sure you don't want a lift?"

He shook his head. "Thank you, but no. There's a job to do here. Who knows how many people over in the town saw that thing last night. I have a feeling there'll be quite a few memories to modify before we get back to London."

Daniel turned to face Ellie, and they stood not quite knowing what to say as the others filed away back into Peg's cottage.

"I'm going to miss you, Ellie Silver. Thank you

for being such a funny, wise, annoying, infuriating, brilliant best friend. I'll look after your dad's shop the best I can."

"It's your shop now," she said. "And I couldn't imagine it belonging to anyone better."

She did something then that he did not expect. She leaned in and planted a kiss on the place where the corner of his mouth met his cheek. He was so stunned that he didn't quite know what to do, or what to say. So he smiled, and walked over to the door of the Nowhere Emporium, looking back at Ellie one more time. The *Book of Wonders* was tucked safely in his coat as he entered the shop, the warmth and smells of dust and polish and dry summer grass wrapping around him.

He'd see Ellie again of course. He knew he would. But things would never be the same. And that was the way of the world, wasn't it? Things changed. Even magic couldn't stop that. And anyway, not all change was bad, was it? Why, only six months ago, Daniel had been a lonely orphan living a miserable life. Where might he be in another six months? Or a year?

The sadness of saying goodbye to Ellie was still there. But something else was keeping it company: excitement. Excitement at the possibility of what might come next.

Daniel went to one of the cabinets, where an old globe sat, and he lifted it down and blew off the thick layer of dust. He spun the globe and stopped it with his finger, examining the spot beneath his fingertip.

"Hmm. Should be interesting."

Daniel went to the instrument on the wall and turned the many dials. Then he went to the fireplace, where the fire always burned, and grabbed the coal bucket. Dipping his hand in, he took some coal, and paused, and smiled. Because he knew that wherever and whenever he might end up, there were friends to come back to, and others to discover.

And who knows, he thought, *maybe one day I'll be able to help someone the way Mr Silver helped me.*

He tossed the coal into the fire. The flames burned dazzling bright and the world lurched.

Off went Daniel Holmes in his Nowhere Emporium, on the trail of adventure.

One day it will be time for Daniel to hand the Nowhere Emporium to someone else.

And so, when the grand old shop made of midnight bricks comes to your town at last, and you push through the door and enter a world of Wonders, it might be wise to ask yourself a question.

Will I be next?

Are you brave?

Read on for an exciting extract from
Ross MacKenzie's mysterious and
magical novel *Shadowsmith*.

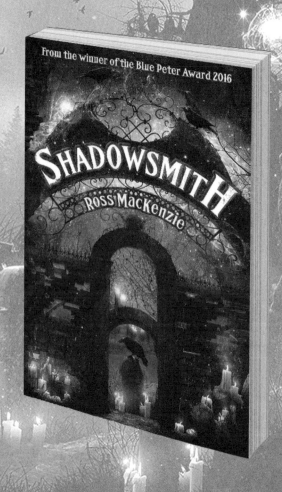

The Girl at
the Window

Kirby lay on his bed and stared at the spider on the ceiling.

It's watching me, he thought as the spider twitched its legs. *It's actually watching me.*

The spider was about the size of a fifty pence piece. It was blacker than black, the colour of a nightmare.

And it had been following him.

He knew it sounded mad. But for the last week it seemed like the spider was everywhere he went. Even when he couldn't see it, he could sense it. And when he thought about the spider, inside his head felt like the air just before a rainstorm, heavy and dull and full.

He was beginning to wonder if it was really there at all. Maybe it was a trick of the mind, his brain's way of distracting him from real life, from the awful thing that was happening to his family.

Two weeks had passed since the storm.

When you lived by the sea you got used to storms. They were a part of life, as normal as shopping or homework or the threat of gull droppings on your ice cream. But this one had been different. Nobody had predicted that such a violent storm would strike at the start of summer. Kirby could still hear the roar of the wind through the winding streets of Craghaven, still see the rain smashing against his classroom window. He could hear his footsteps echo in the empty school corridors and see the frightened look in his dad's eyes as he waited for Kirby in the office.

Two weeks.

The summer holidays had begun since then. His classmates were out playing in the streets or heading off on holiday with their families, full of nervous excitement at the thought of starting high school at the end of the summer. Repair work had begun on the storm-damaged buildings. The world was still turning. Life was going on.

But not for Kirby or his dad.

For them, the world would not turn again until the moment Mum woke up.

The dread of never seeing her smile again, never hearing her voice or feeling one of her hugs had consumed Kirby, filled him up until there was room for nothing else.

Until the spider had arrived.

Clack!

Kirby's gaze left the spider, flicked to the window.

Clack!

He sat up just as another stone – *clack!* – bounced off the window pane.

There was a girl in a yellow plastic raincoat down on the pavement. When she spotted him peering out at her, she smiled and waved, and motioned for him to open the window.

Kirby poked his head out into the night. "Who're you?" he said. Then, trying to sound stern like his dad, he added, "What you playing at?"

"I'm Amelia," said the girl in the raincoat. "Amelia Pigeon. And I'm not playing. I'm not playing at all." Amelia Pigeon half closed her eyes. "Are you brave?"

Kirby frowned. Am I brave? What a weird question.

Funny though – he'd been asking himself the same thing a lot lately.

"Dunno," he said. "Hope so."

Amelia Pigeon smiled up at him, all front teeth and freckles. She looked about twelve, the same age as Kirby. "That's a good answer. Usually I find it's the ones who strut around with their chests puffed out that aren't brave at all. Not when it matters." She tilted her head to one side. "You've seen the spiders, haven't you?"

Kirby's breath caught in his throat. "There's more than one?"

"Course there's more," said Amelia. "When did you see one last?"

"A minute ago. It's gone."

Amelia shook her head. "Not gone. Never gone. Just watching."

"Watching what?"

Amelia scratched her nose. "You. They want you gone."

"You do know that's crazy?" said Kirby.

"Think that if you want," said Amelia with a shrug. "Won't make the slightest bit of difference. Can anyone else in your house see them?"

"Don't think so. Dad hates spiders. If he'd seen one I'd have heard him swearing at it or trying to kill it with one of his shoes. When you say they want me gone…"

"Dead," said Amelia matter-of-factly. "They want you dead. I said gone because it sounds less scary."

Kirby was not usually the type of boy to be left stuck for words. But now he thought for a moment and opened his mouth, and all he could say was, "What?"

Amelia Pigeon reached into her yellow raincoat, and when she pulled out her hand she was holding a rough, barky twig about the length of a ruler. "Take this," she said, and she tossed it up to the window. Kirby missed it. Amelia Pigeon gave him a sharp look and tossed it again. This time he caught it.

"What is it?"

"Hazel. Picked at midnight. Simple, but it works."

Kirby examined the stick. It looked like every other stick he'd ever seen.

"They'll come soon," said Amelia. "Don't know exactly when. But they'll come. And there'll be lots of 'em."

"Lots of spiders?"

"When they come, use the hazel," Amelia went on. "Like this…" She pulled another twig from the depths of her raincoat, touched the tip to the ground, and drew an imaginary circle around herself. "They won't come inside the circle. Whatever you do, don't step outside it. And don't panic."

"But—"

"I have to go. Things I need to do. I'll be back."

"If you say so," said Kirby. He glanced at the hazel twig in his hand, and when he looked back the girl was gone.

THE STORY CONTINUES IN

MEET ROSS MACKENZIE

The multi-award-winning author of *The Nowhere Emporium, The Elsewhere Emporium* and *Shadowsmith*. He lives in Renfrew, Scotland where he grew up, with his wife and two daughters, but spends much of his time in another world.

Daniel puts his own spin on the Emporium after taking over from Mr Silver. What gave you the idea to change the shop?

I think the Emporium reflects the personality of the person in charge. Mr Silver's Emporium was dark and mysterious like the man himself. Daniel's wonder and amazement and playfulness shine through – I thought the Carnival was a great way to encompass that.

What's the best idea for a Wonder that you've heard from a reader?

There have been some amazing suggestions so this is very difficult to answer! The one that always sticks out – probably because so many people can relate – is the girl who said she'd create a room that would make her little brother less annoying. Genius!

We meet a whole host of new characters in *The Elsewhere Emporium*. Which one is your favourite?

Mrs Hennypeck without a doubt. She was a lot of fun to write. She may have a temper and a sharp tongue, but she has a good heart and an amazing sense of humour – particularly about the fact that she's dead!

Mr Ivy says that "magicians these days just couldn't create magic this special any more" – do you think that's true?

I've always imagined in the Nowhere Emporium universe that we're witnessing the last throes of a once-great magical world. I don't think it'll ever return to full strength, but very occasionally someone special may come along – Lucien Silver for instance…